Dear Parent:

Psst . . . you're looking at the Super Secret Weapon of Reading. It's called comics.

STEP INTO READING® COMIC READERS are a perfect step in learning to read. They provide visual cues to the meaning of words and helpfully break out short pieces of dialogue into speech balloons.

Here are some terms commonly associated with comics:
   PANEL: A section of a comic with a box drawn around it.
   CAPTION: Narration that helps set the scene.
   SPEECH BALLOON: A bubble containing dialogue.
   GUTTER: The space between panels.

Tips for reading comics with your child:

• Have your child read the speech balloons while you read the captions.
• Ask your child: What is a character feeling? How can you tell?
• Have your child draw a comic showing what happens after the book is finished.

STEP INTO READING® COMIC READERS are designed to engage and to provide an empowering reading experience. They are also fun. The best-kept secret of comics is that they create lifelong readers. And that will make you the real hero of the story!

Jennifer L. Holm and Matthew Holm
Co-creators of the Babymouse and Squish series

For Kasper

RHUS30394

 Published in the United States by Random House Children's Books, a division of Random House LLC, 1745 Broadway, New York, NY 10019, and in Canada by Random House of Canada Limited, Toronto, Penguin Random House Companies.

Visit us on the Web!
StepIntoReading.com
randomhouse.com/kids
dckids.kidswb.com

Educators and librarians, for a variety of teaching tools, visit us at RHTeachersLibrarians.com

ISBN 978-0-385-37403-3 (trade) – ISBN 978-0-385-37404-0 (lib. bdg.) –
ISBN 978-0-385-37405-7 (ebook)
Printed in the United States of America
10 9 8 7 6 5 4 3

STEP INTO READING®

STEP 2

DC SUPER FRIENDS™

A COMIC READER

REPTILE RUMBLE!

By Billy Wrecks

Illustrated by Erik Doescher

Random House 🏠 New York

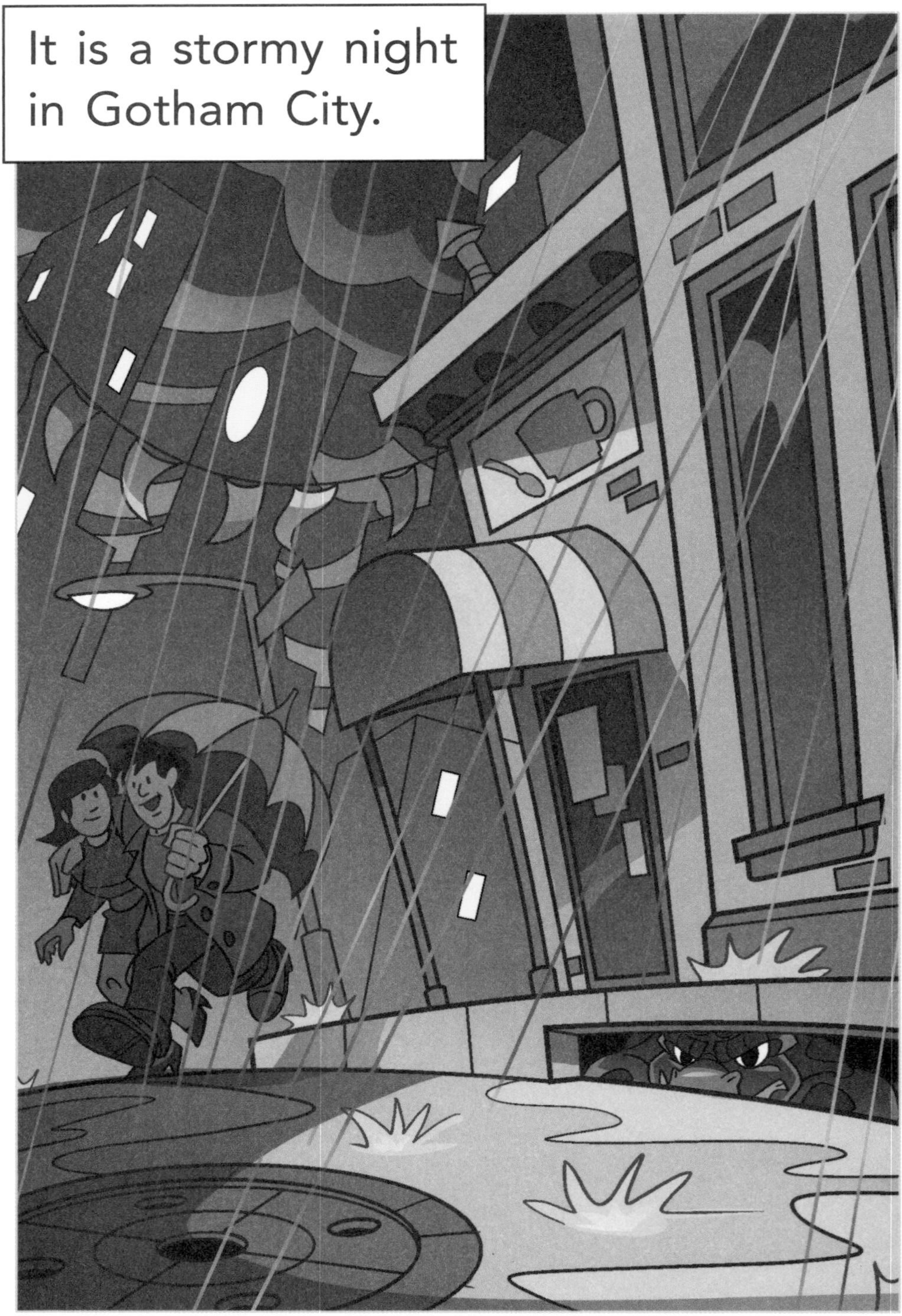
It is a stormy night in Gotham City.

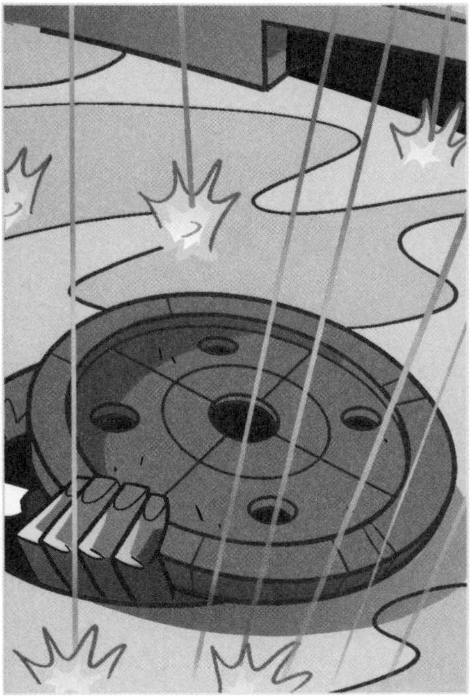

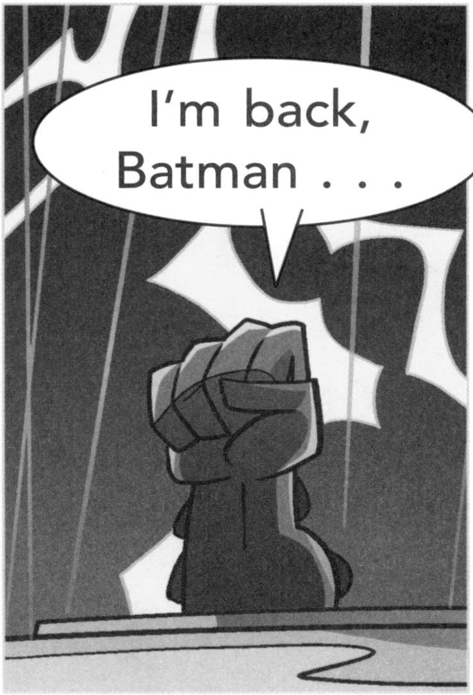
I'm back,
Batman . . .

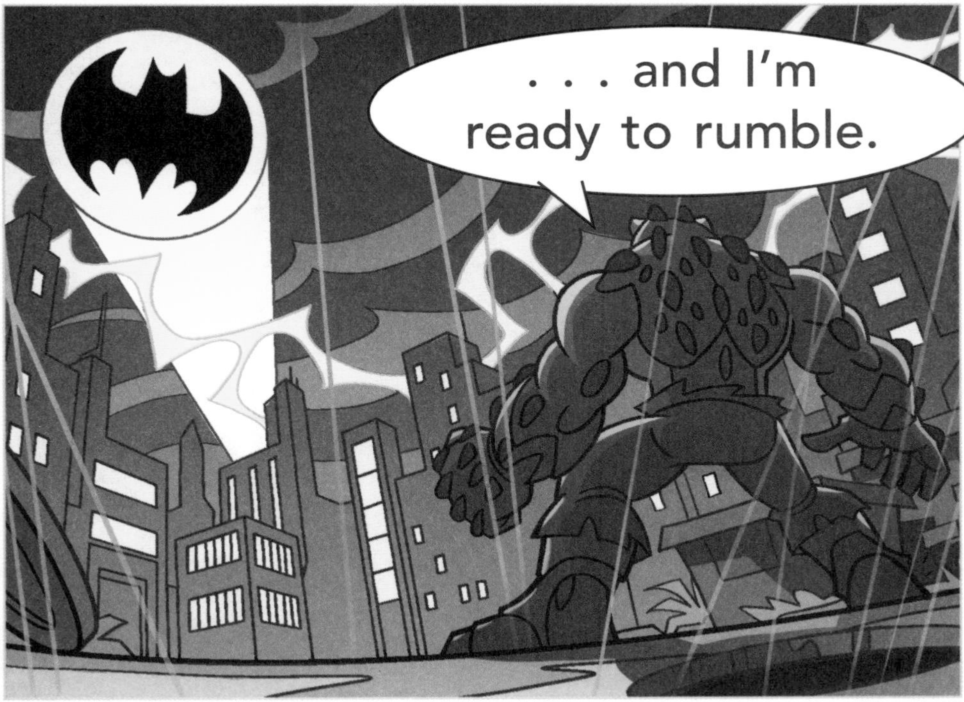
. . . and I'm
ready to rumble.

The next day, a bank car is robbed.

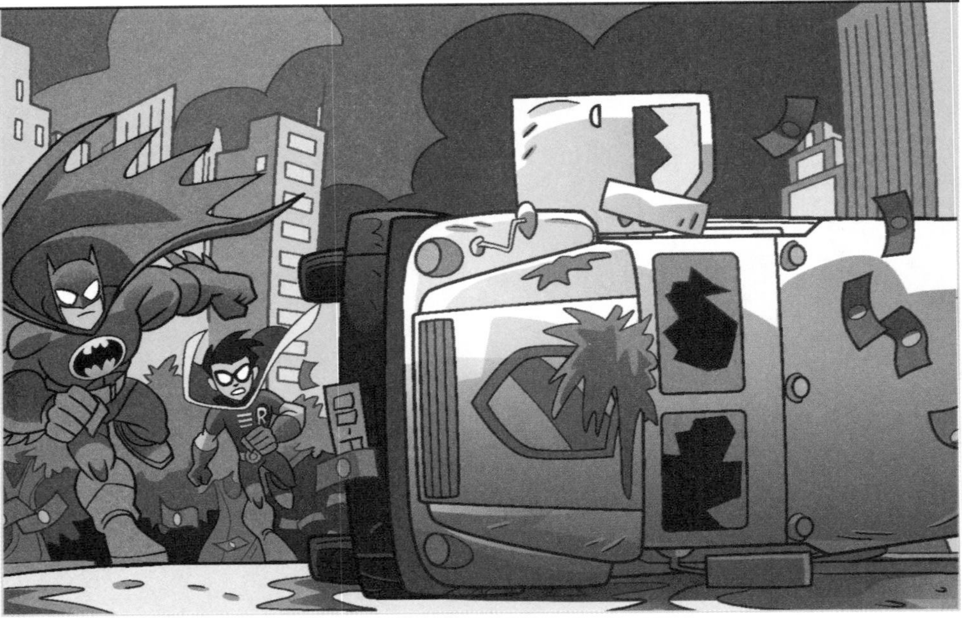

Batman and Robin
look for clues.

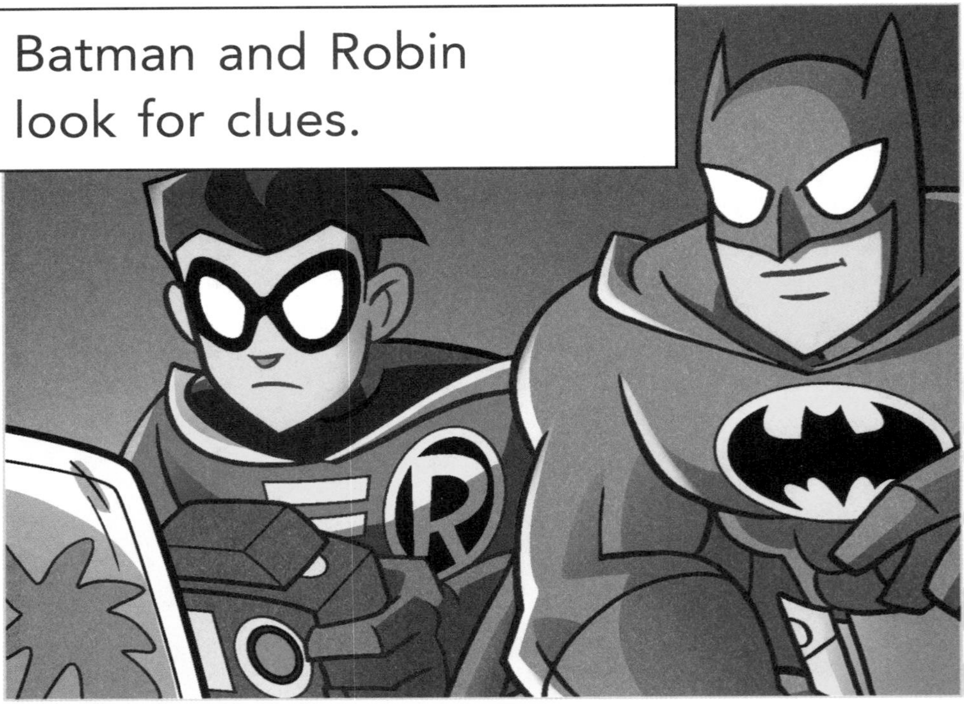

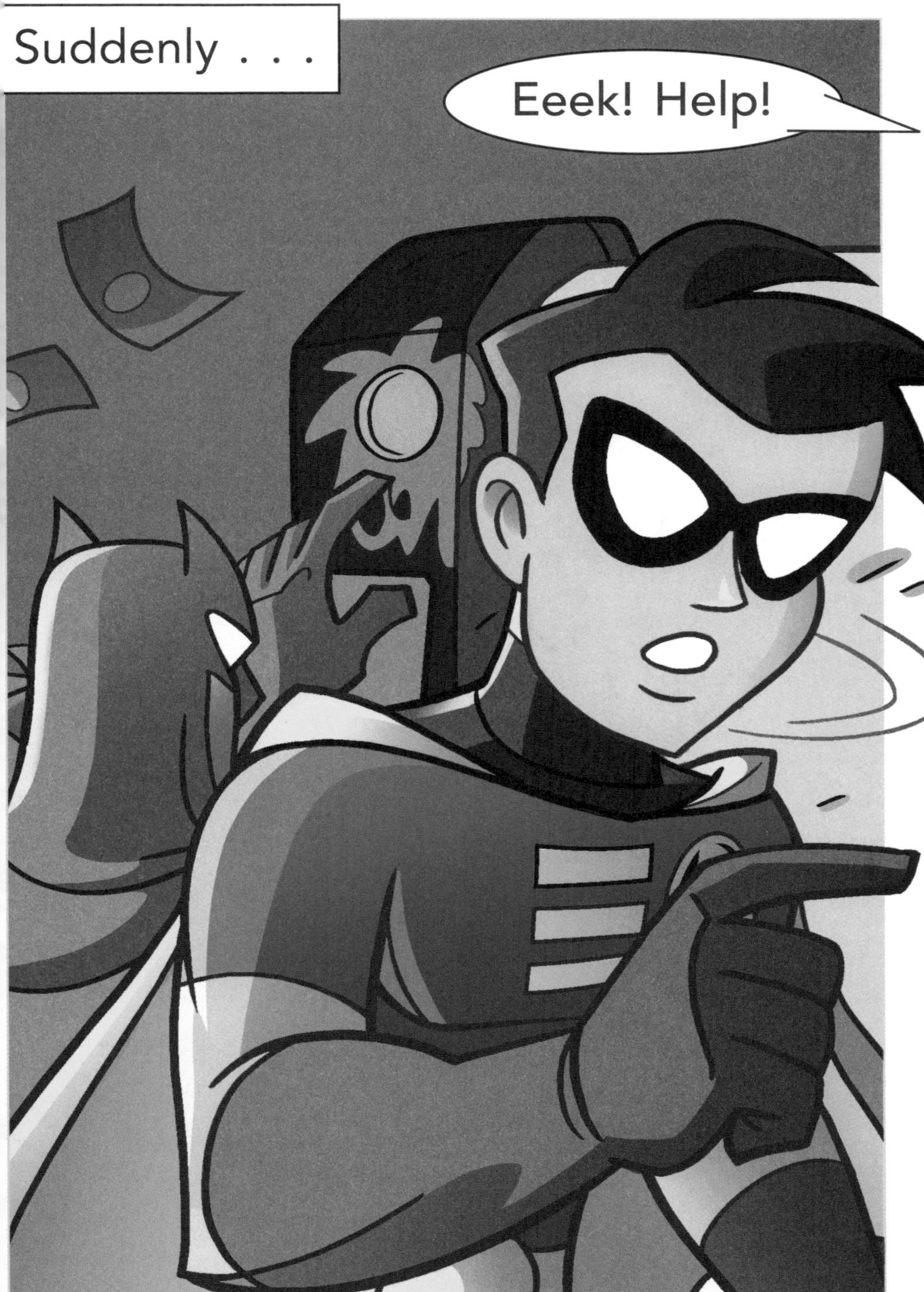
Suddenly . . .
Eeek! Help!

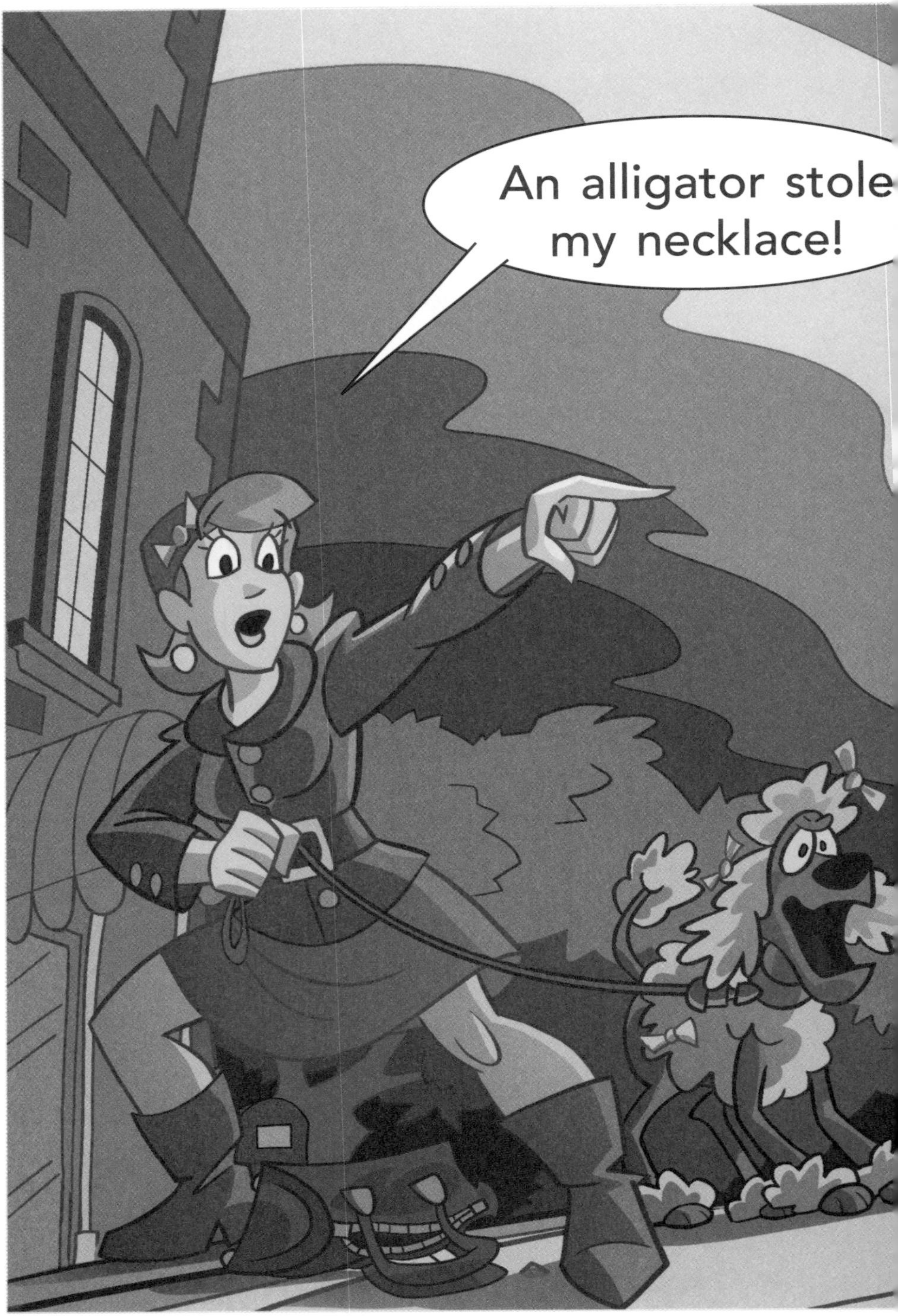
An alligator stole my necklace!

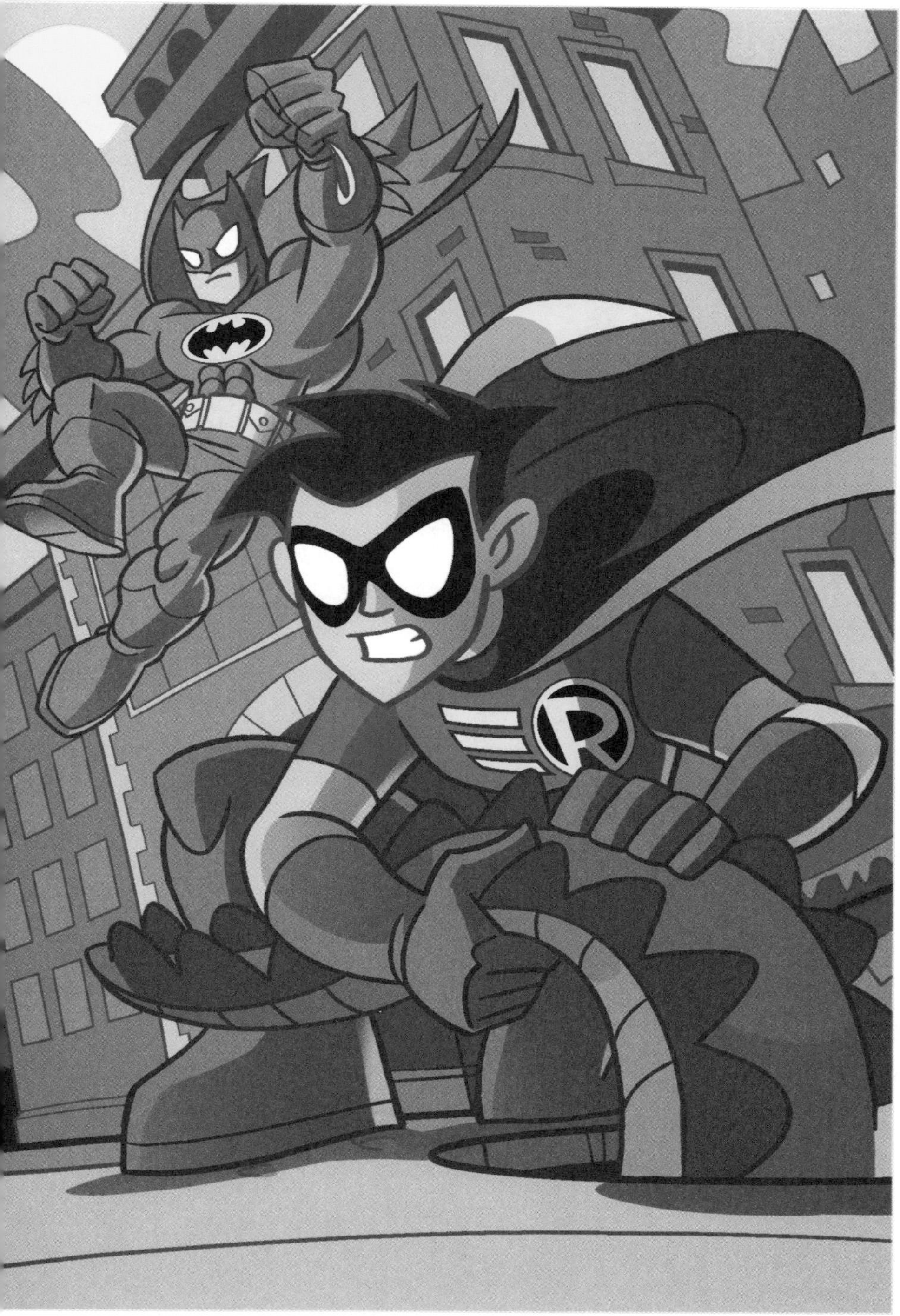

Reports of reptile robberies come in from all across Gotham City.

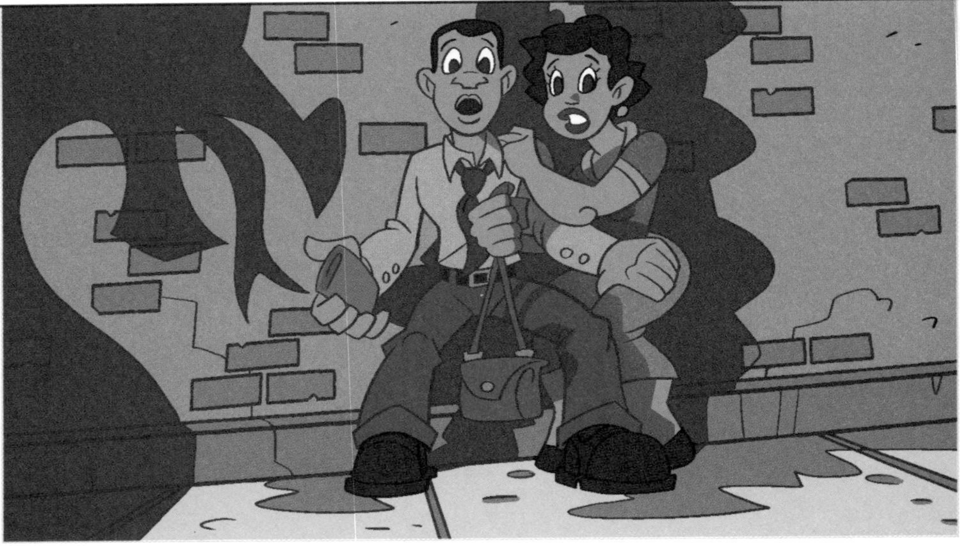

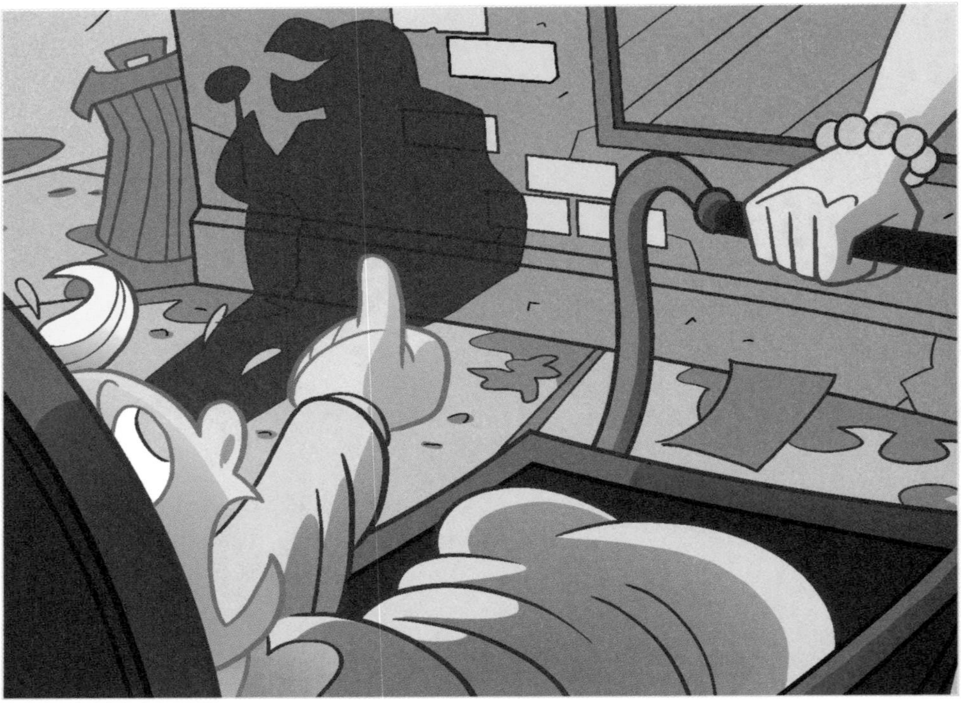

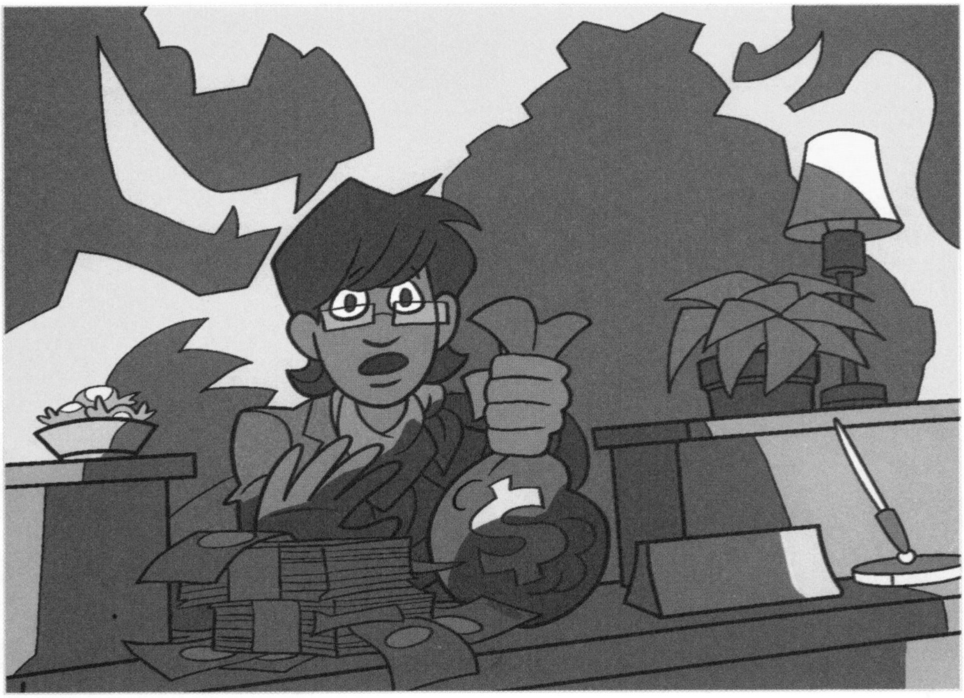

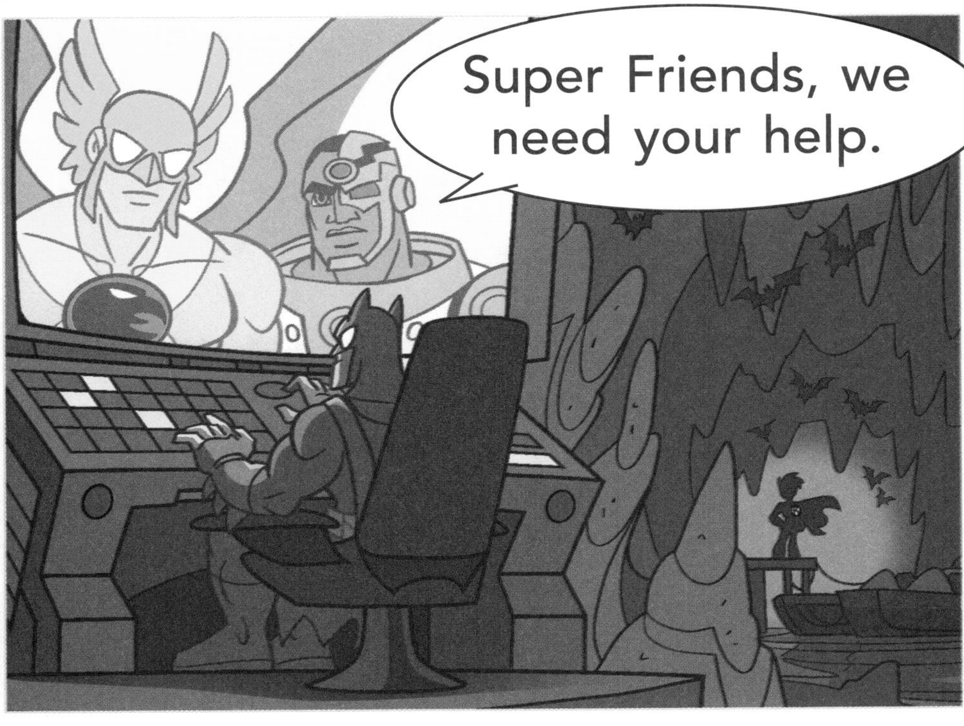
Super Friends, we need your help.

The Batboat roars into the sewer.

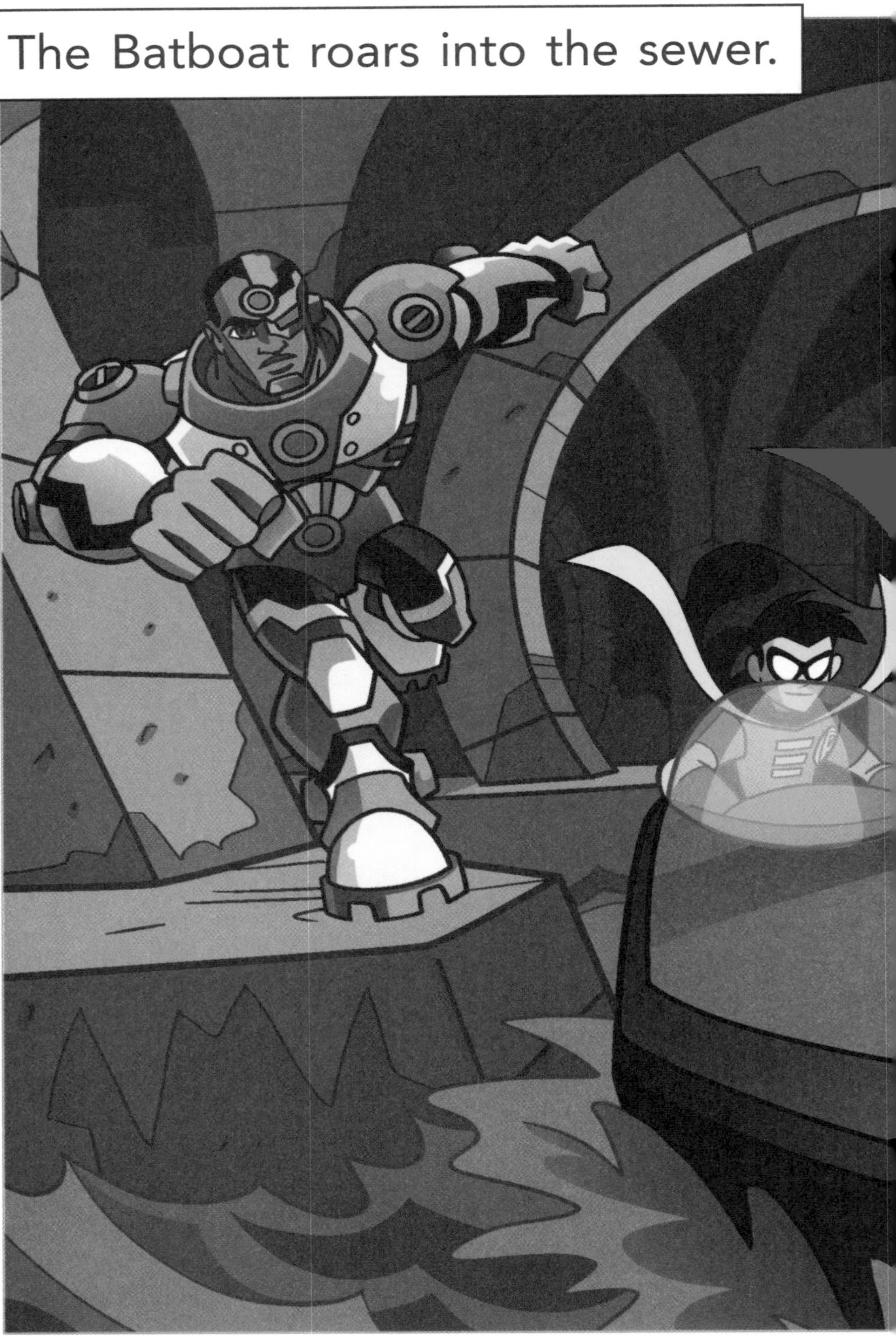

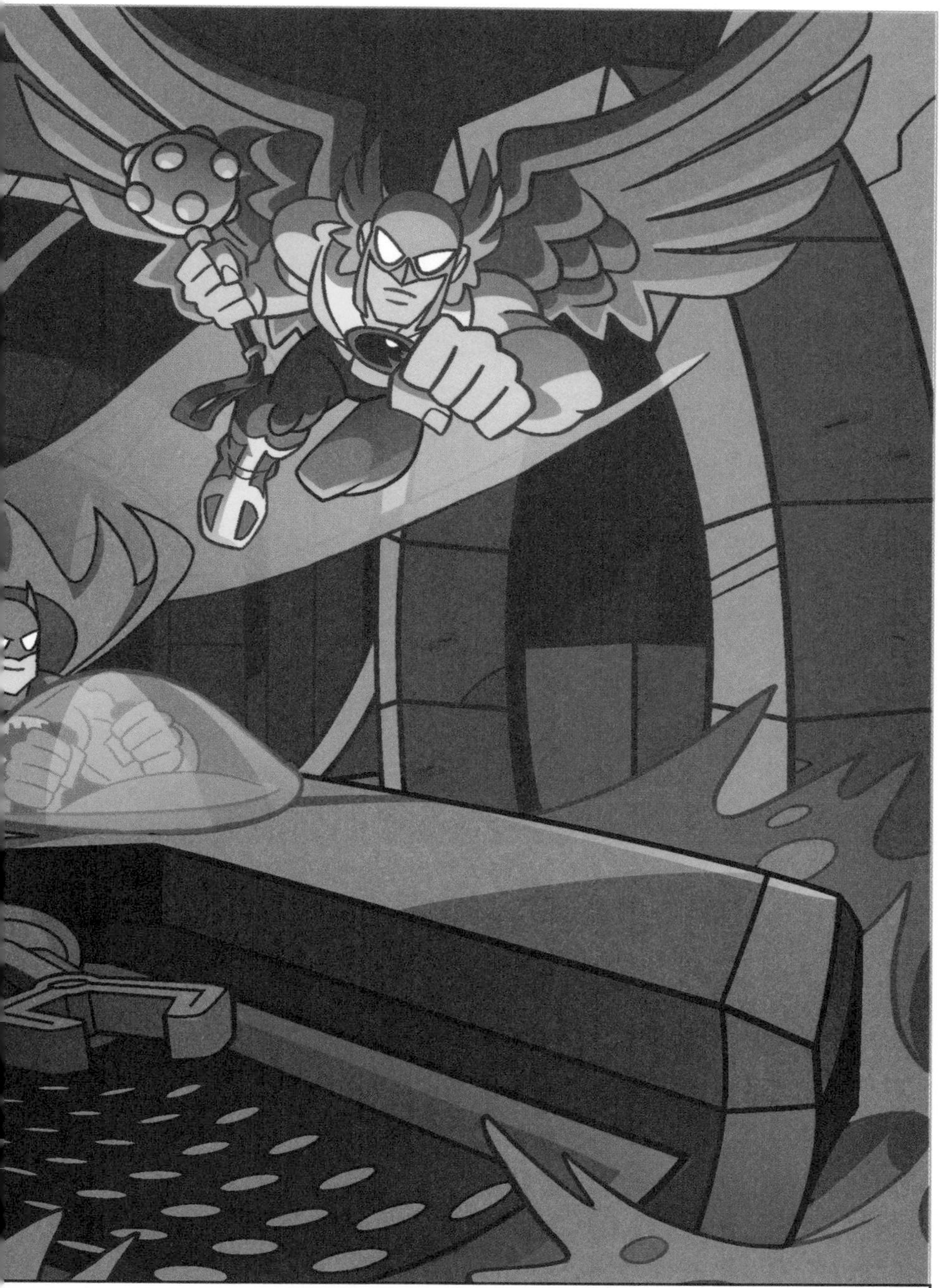

Cyborg and Hawkman follow.

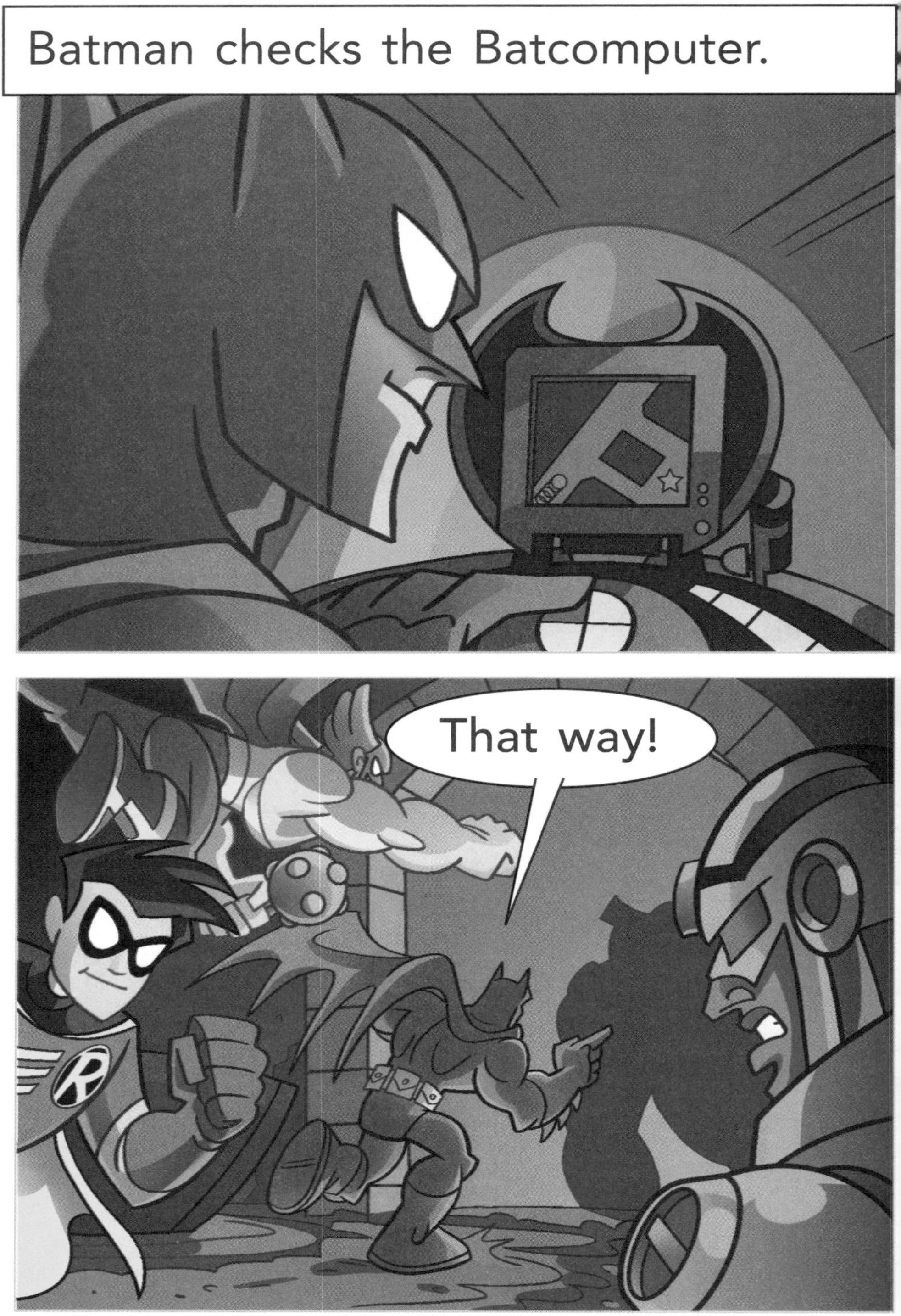
Batman checks the Batcomputer.
That way!

It's the bad guy called Croc!

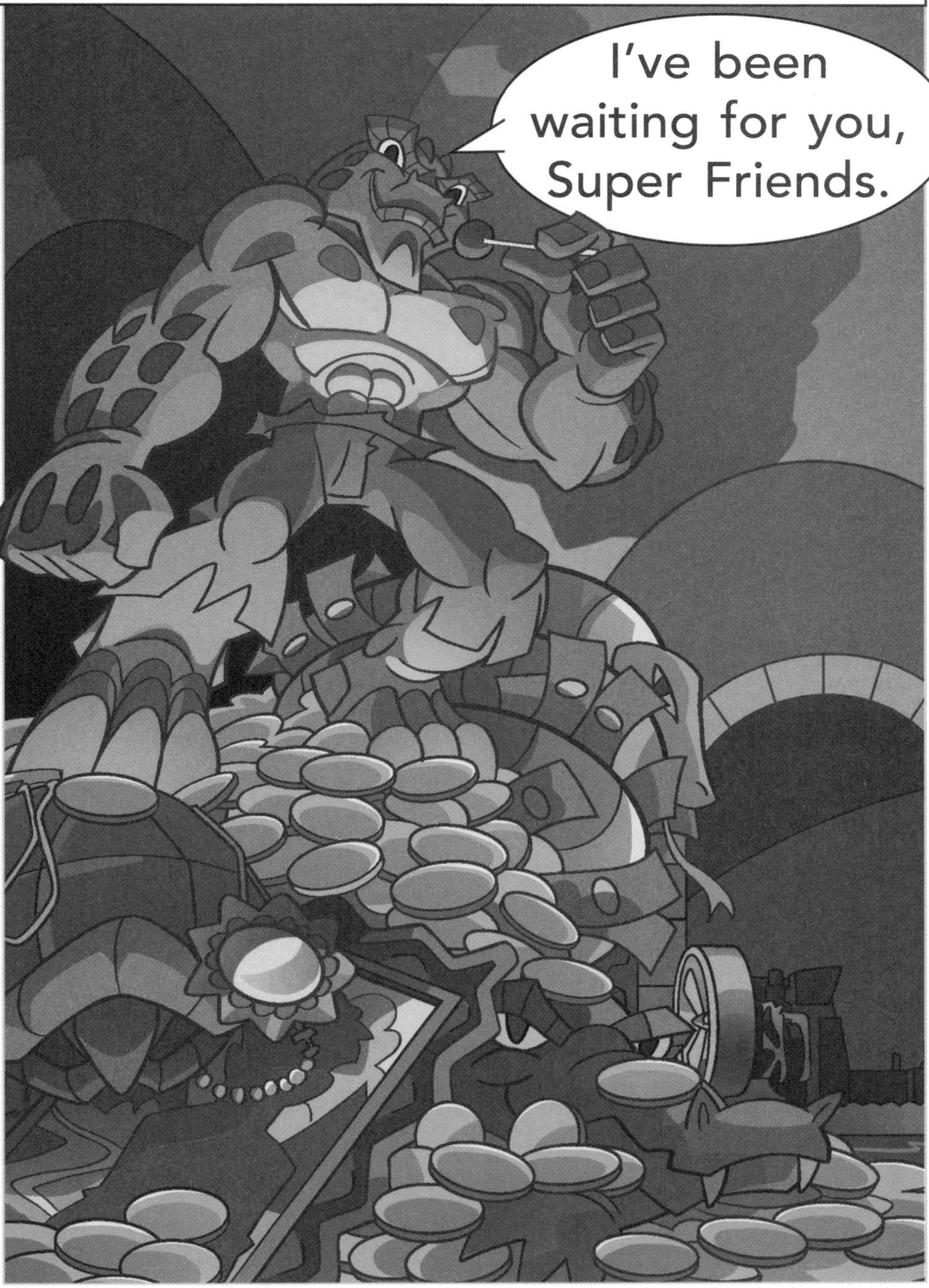
I've been waiting for you, Super Friends.

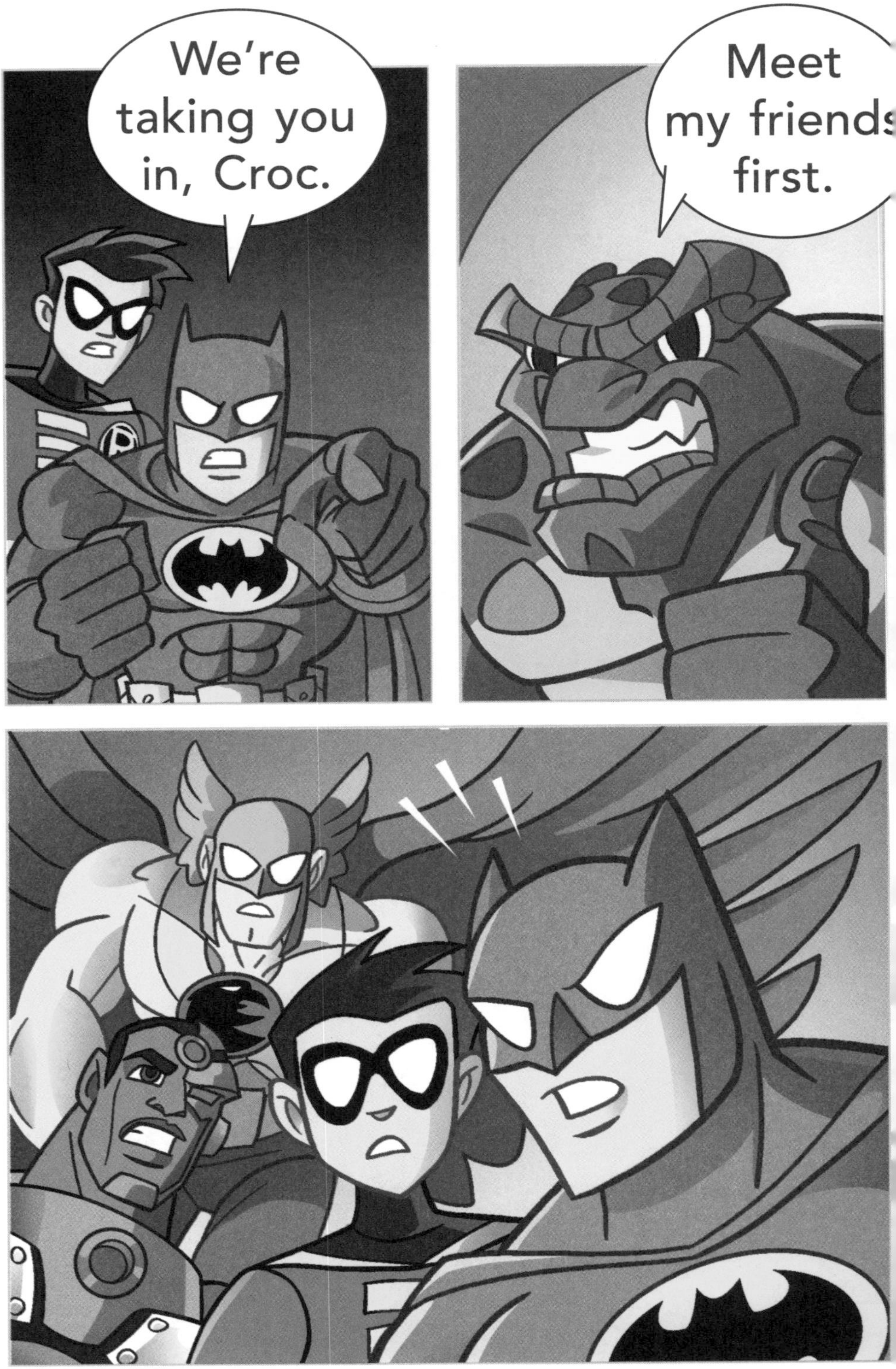
We're taking you in, Croc.
Meet my friends first.

Croc's crew of creatures surprises the Super Friends!

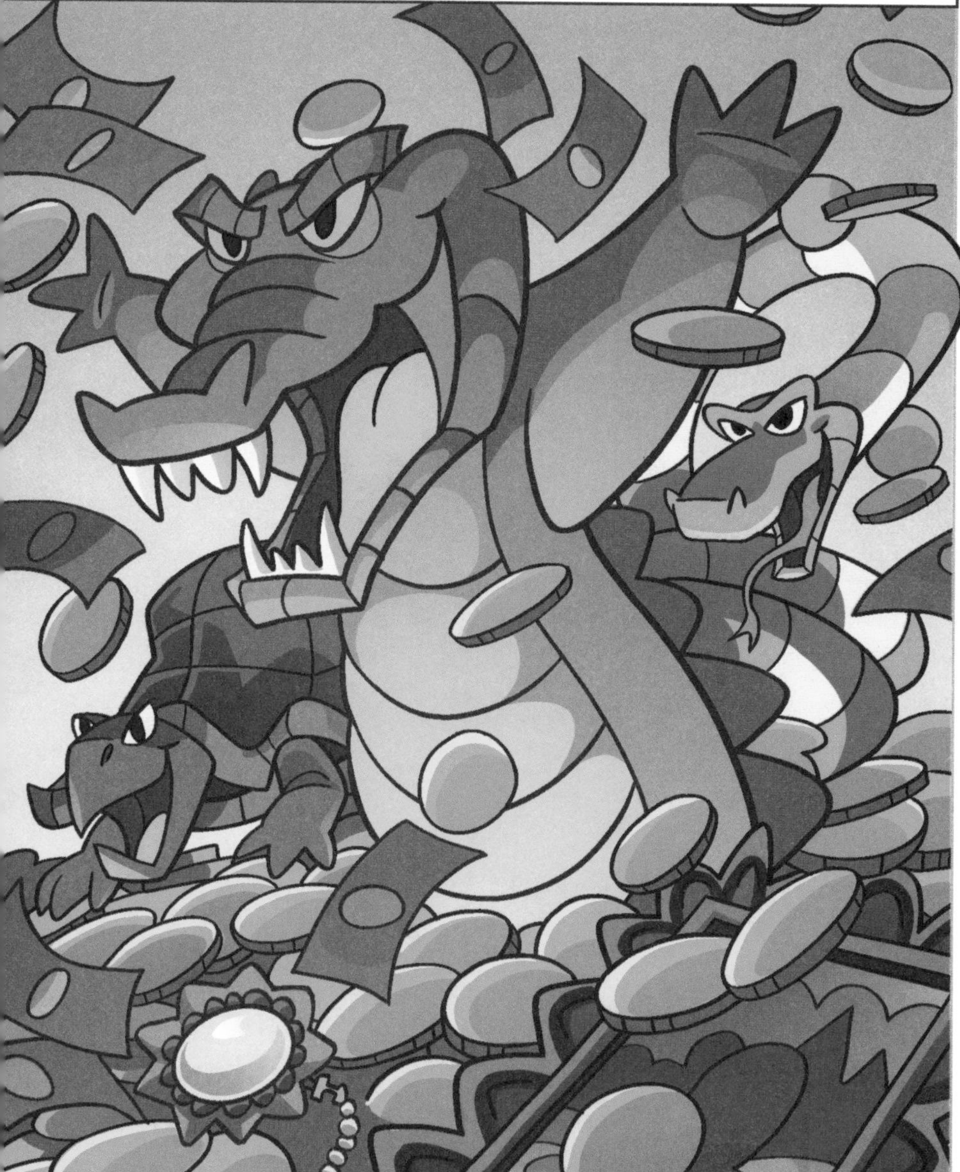

The reptiles attack the Super Friends.
It's a reptile rumble!

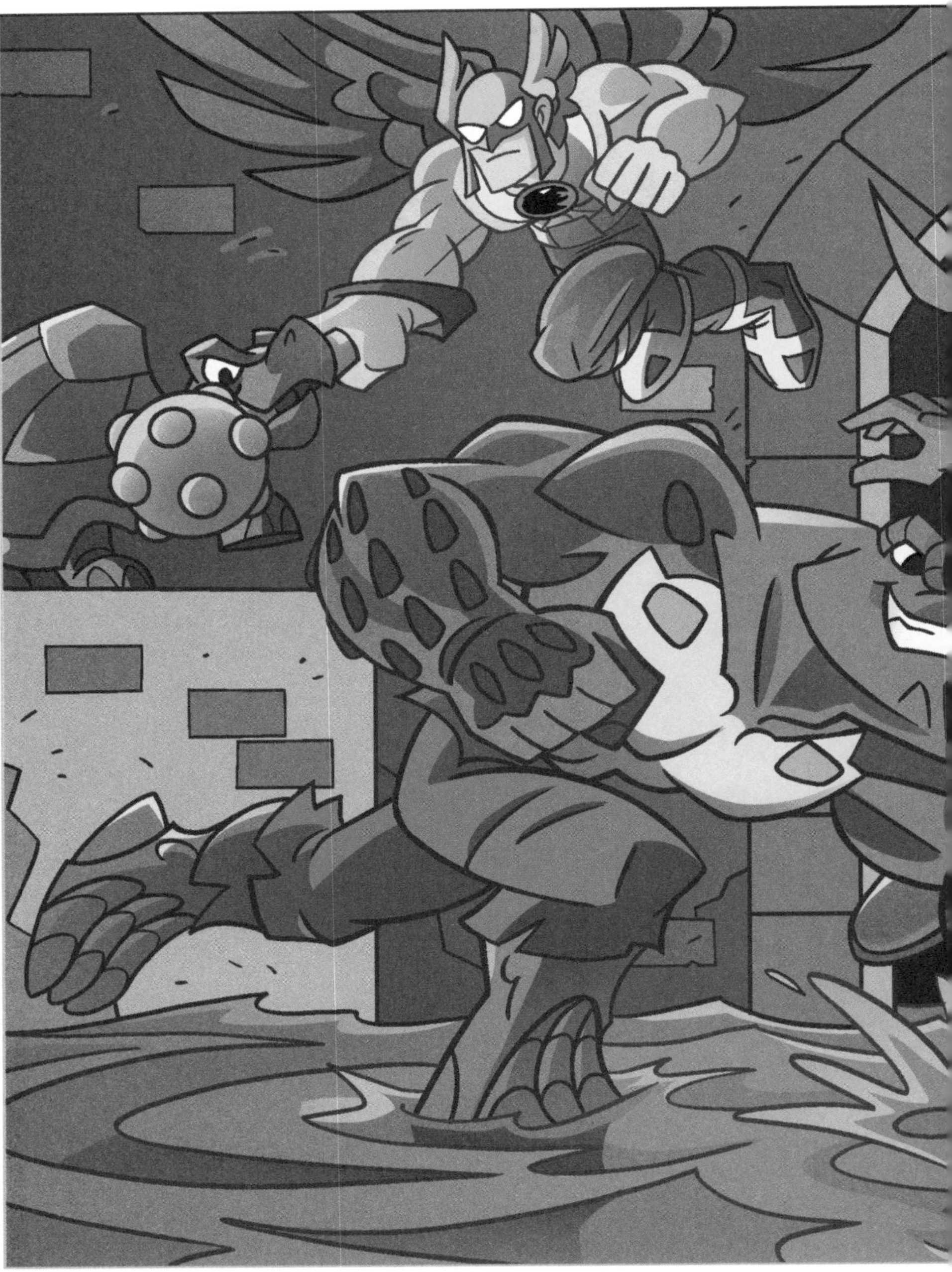

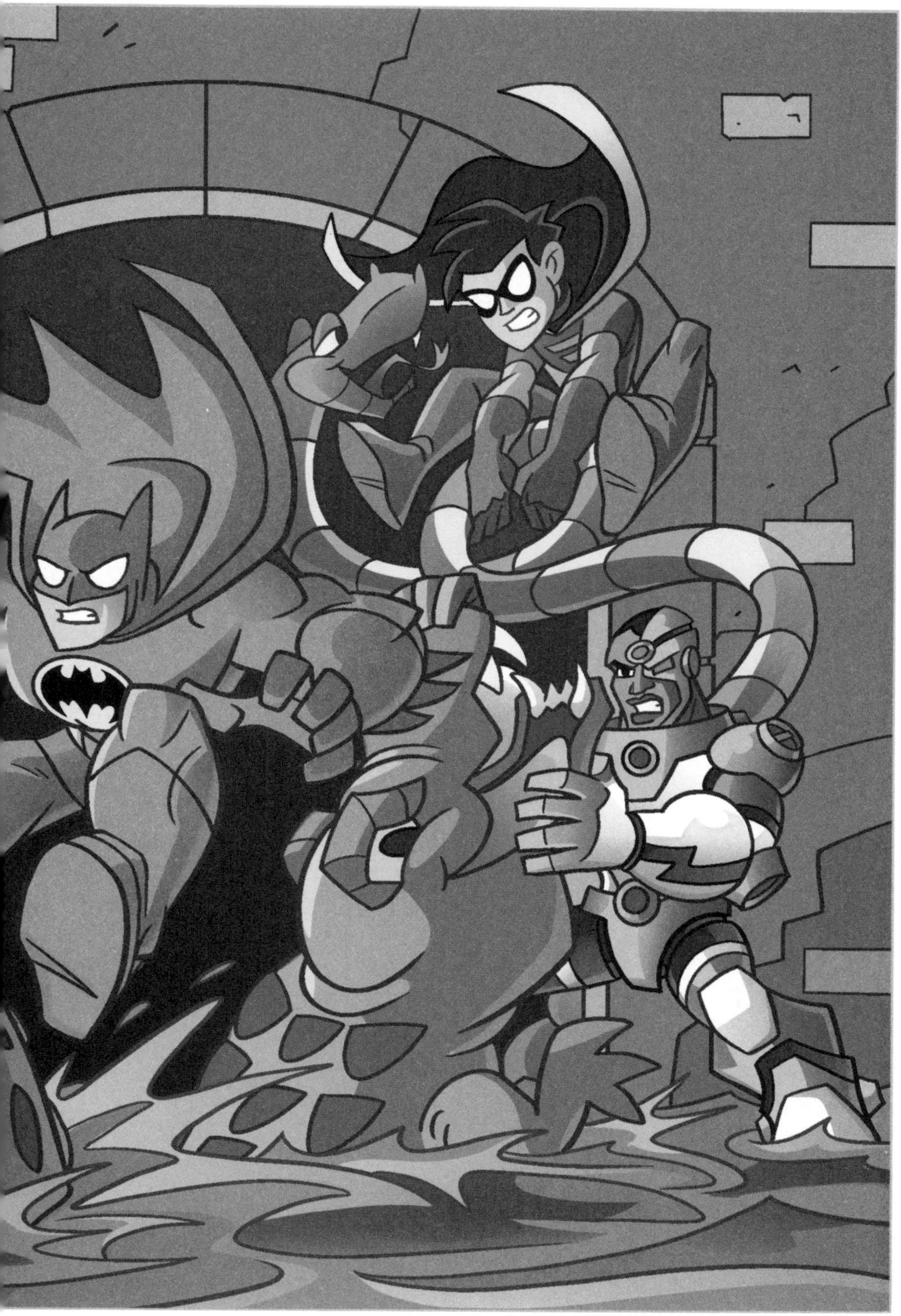

Hawkman flips the turtle on its back.

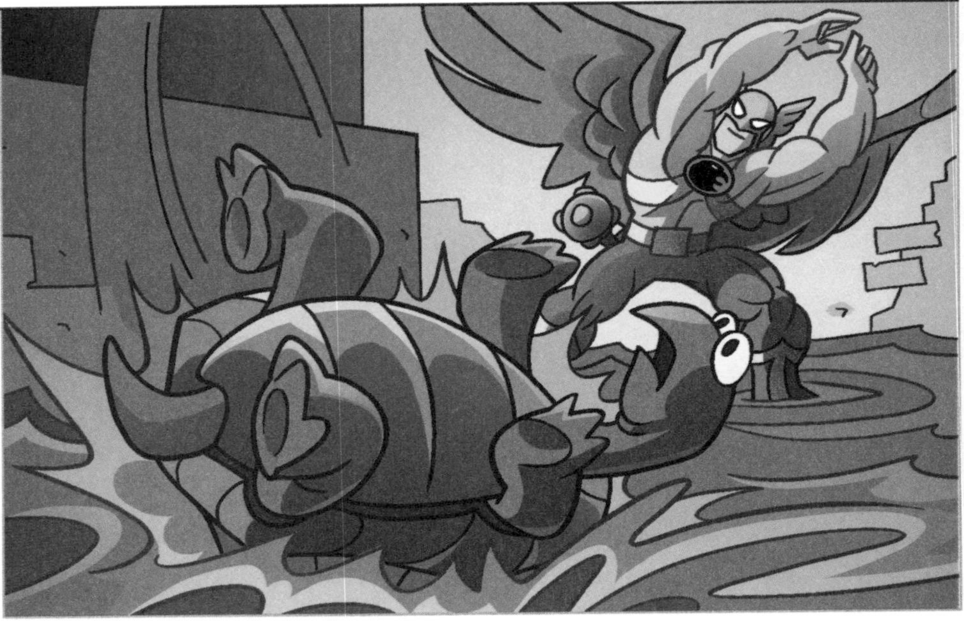

Cyborg seals the alligator's jaws closed.

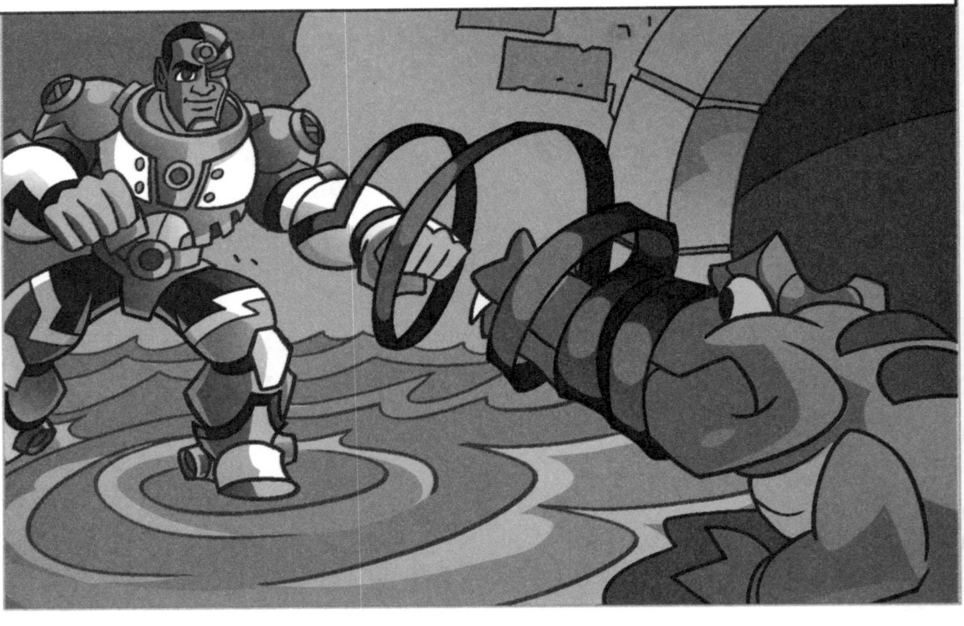

Robin charms the snake.

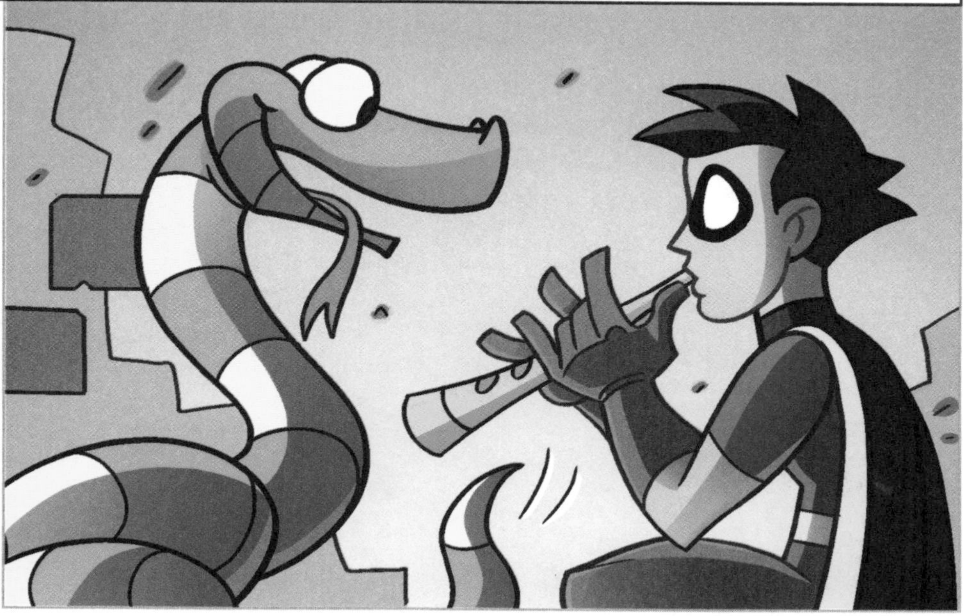

Batman lassos Croc.

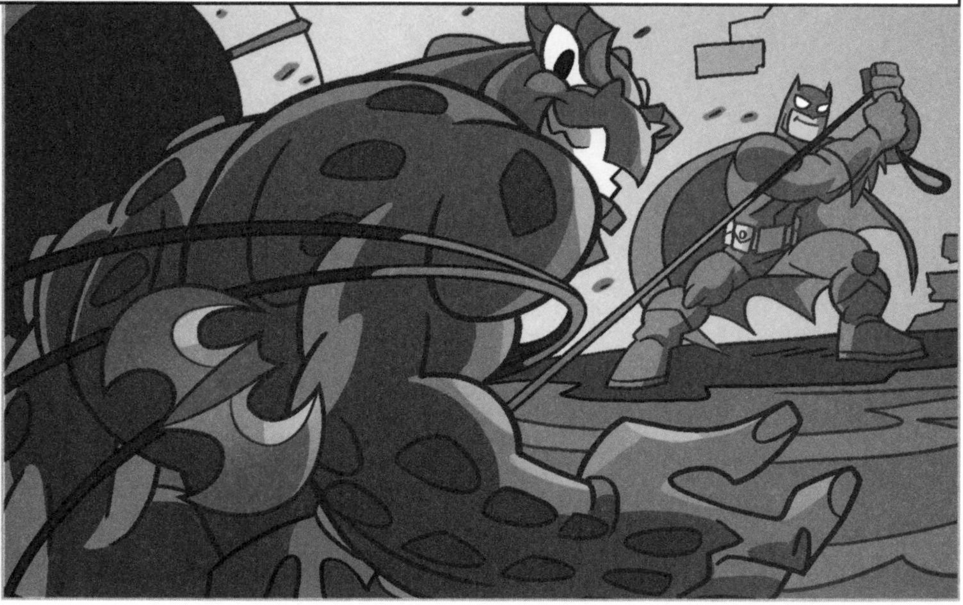

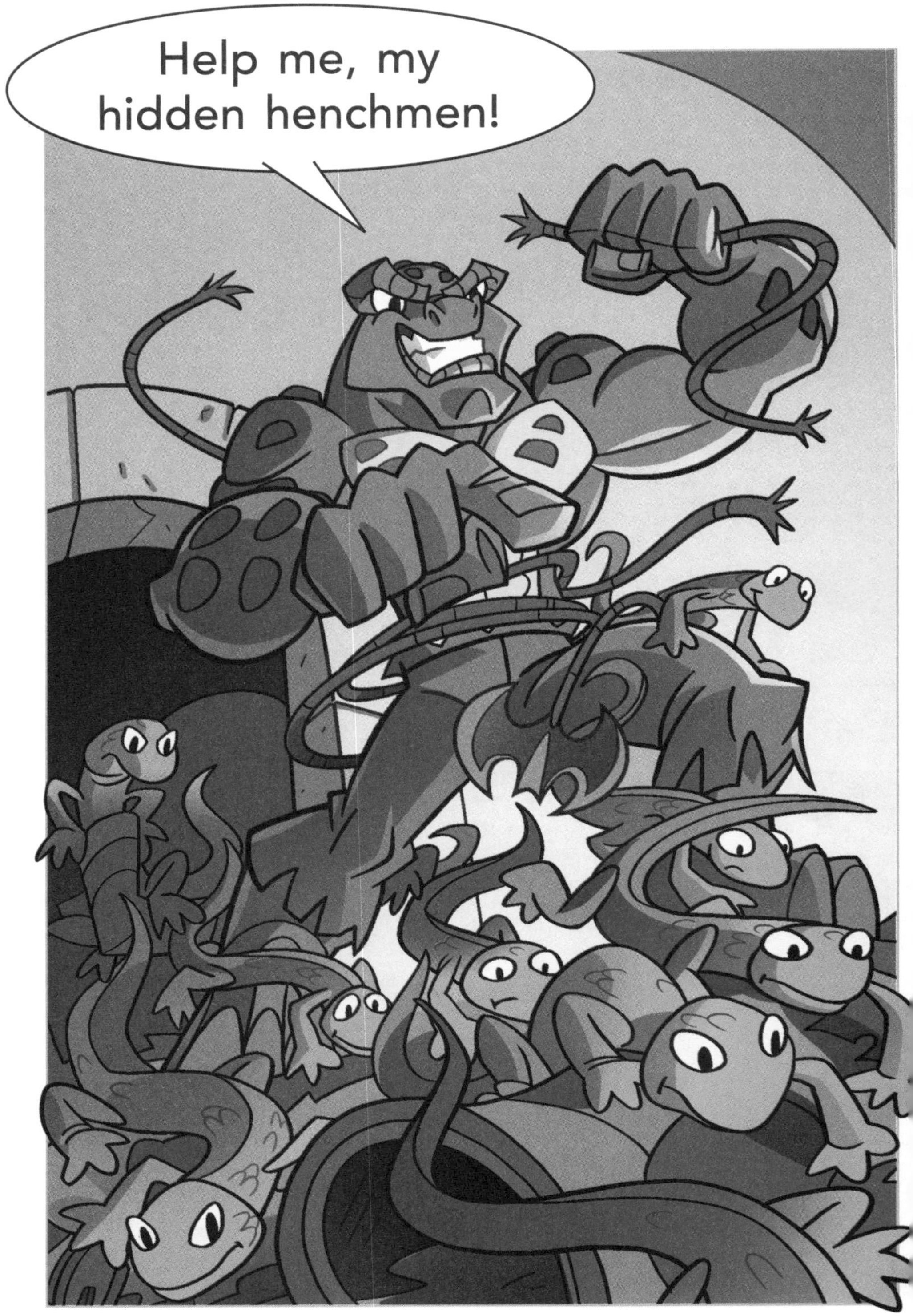
Help me, my hidden henchmen!

The chameleons distract the heroes.

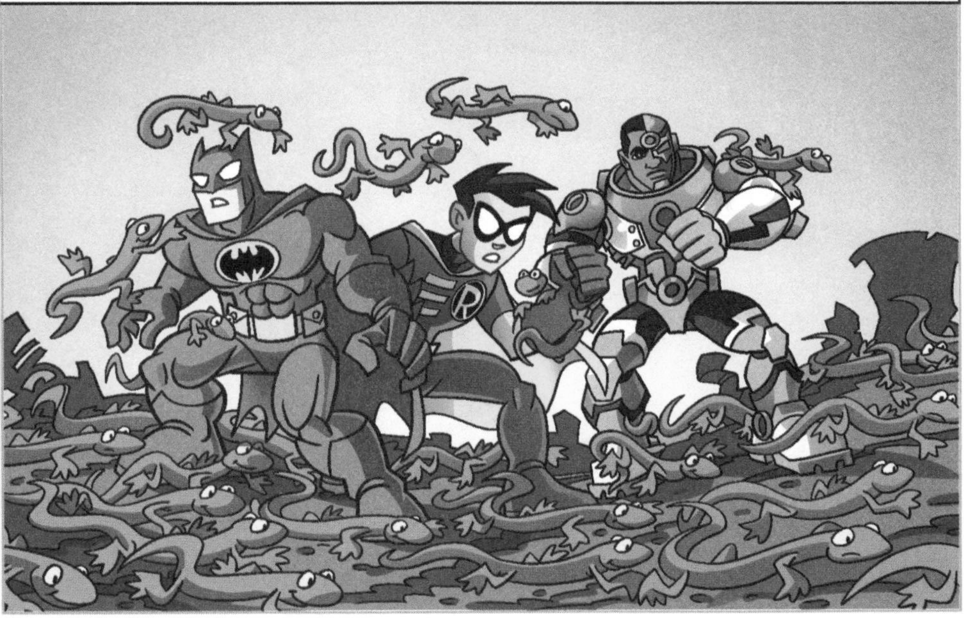

Croc escapes in his airboat.

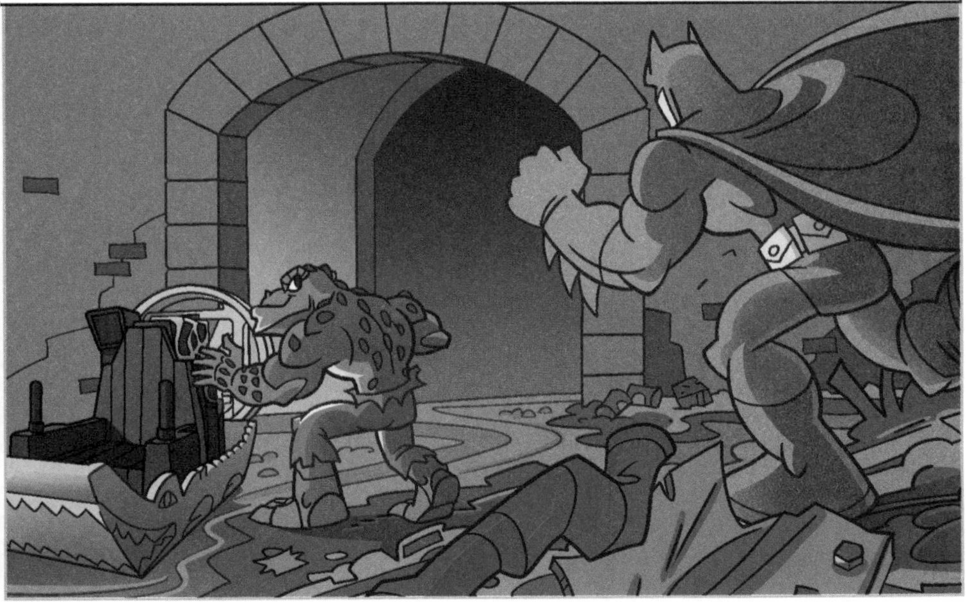

Batman follows Croc in the Batboat.

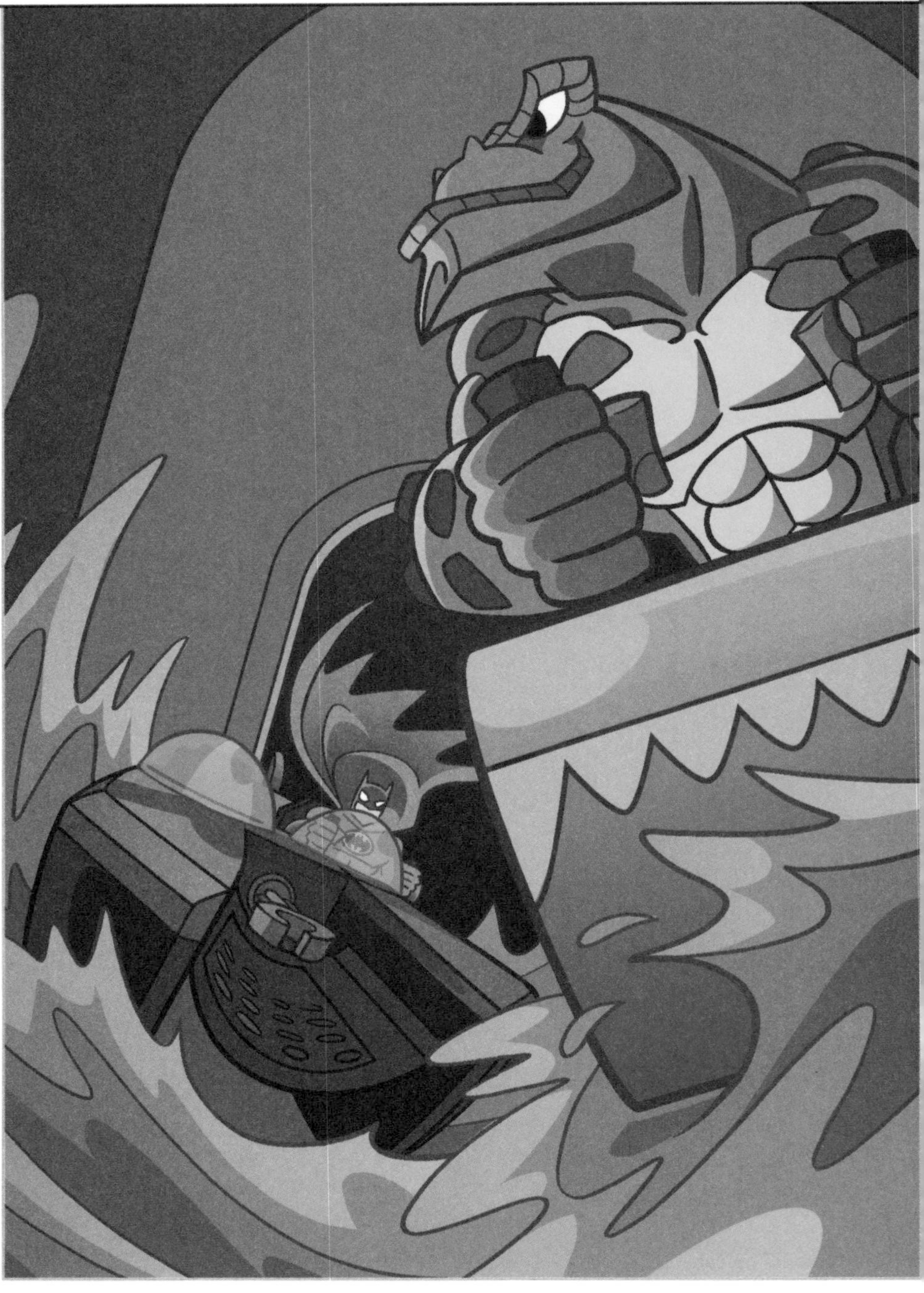

He chases Croc through the sewer.

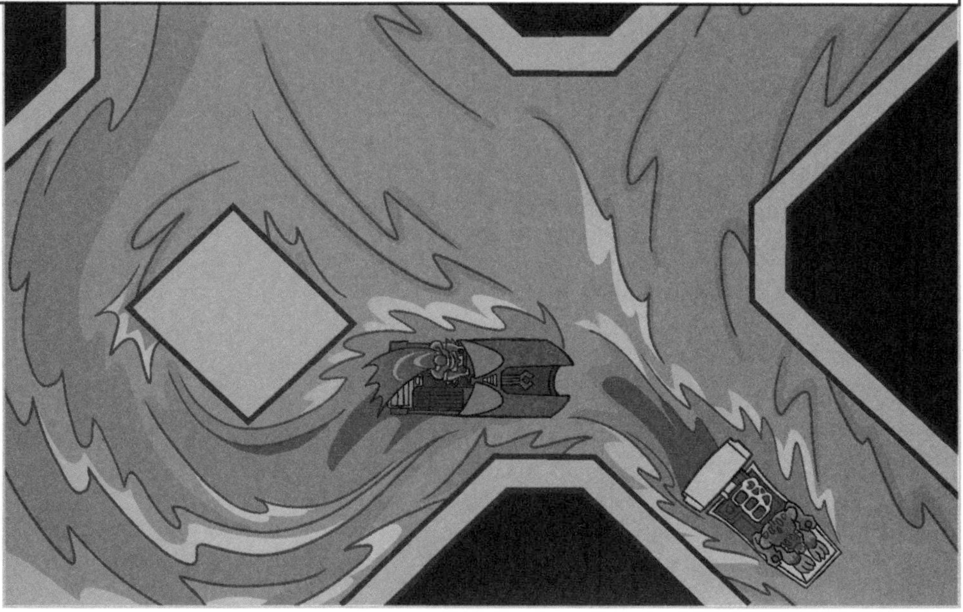

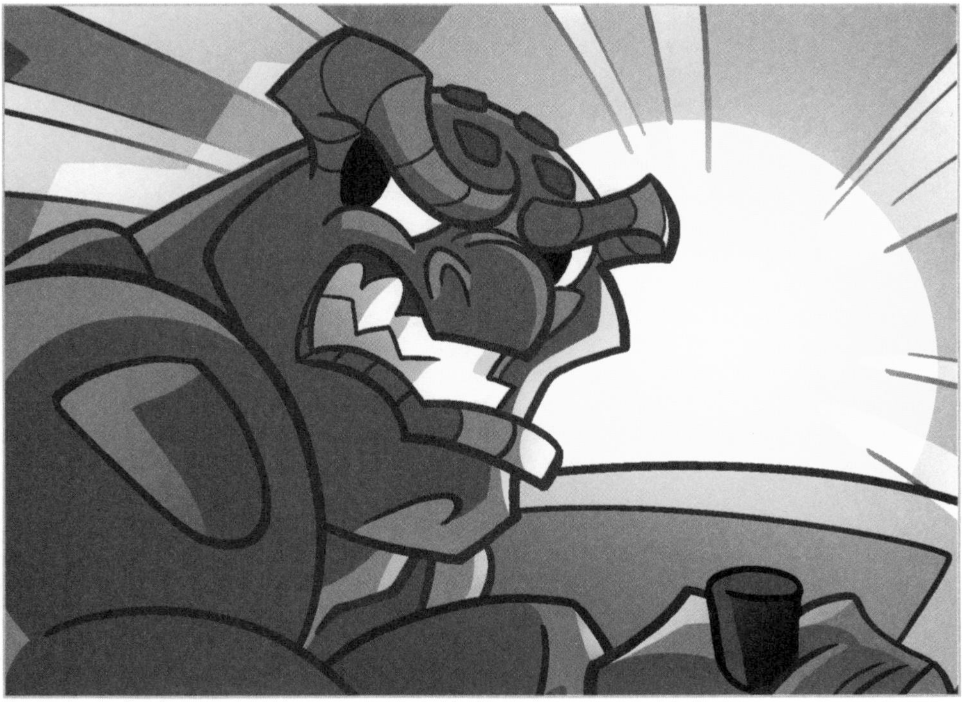

Croc leads Batman into the swamp.

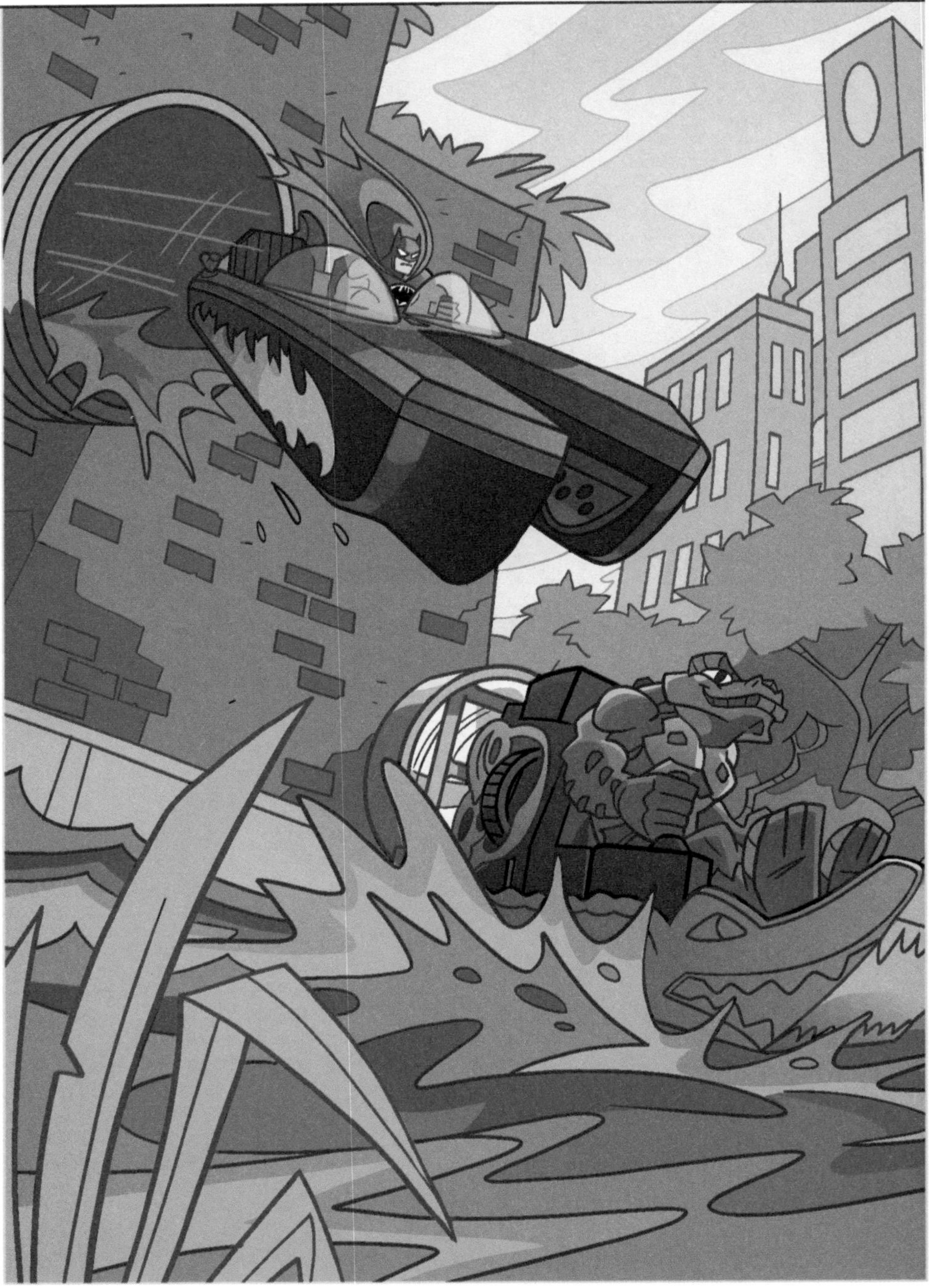

The Batboat gets bogged down.

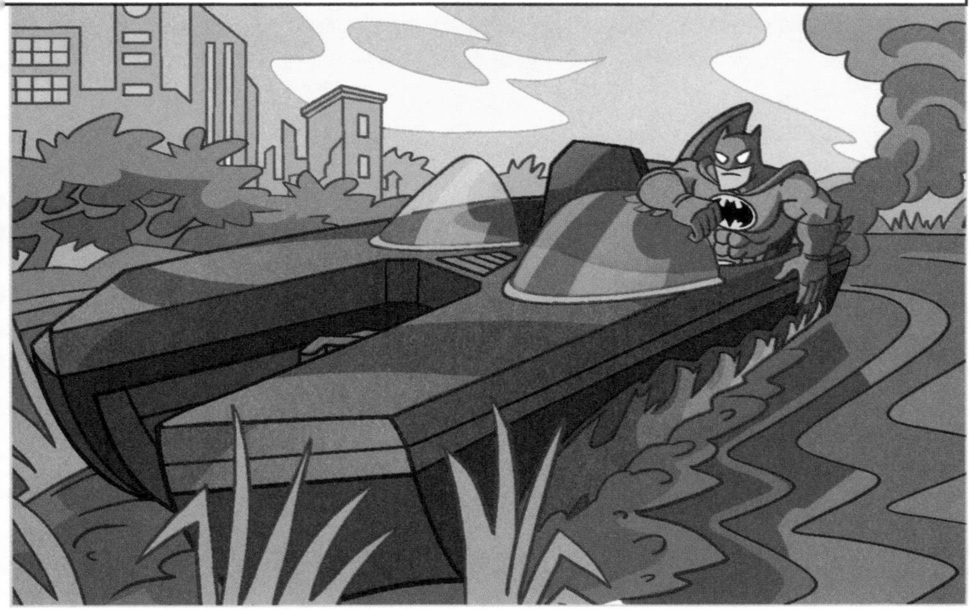

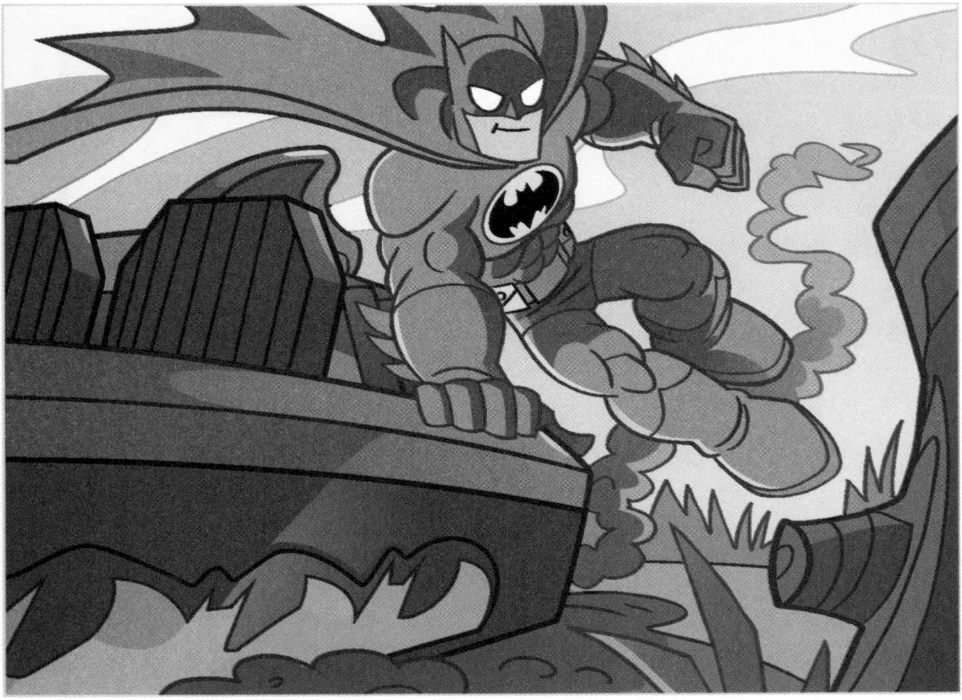

Croc turns his airboat around.

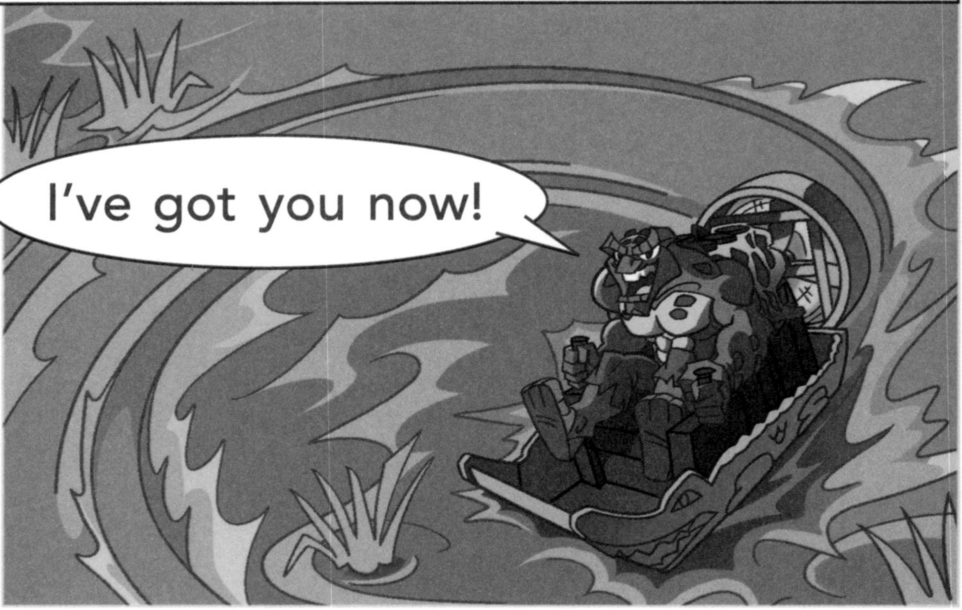
I've got you now!

He charges at Batman!

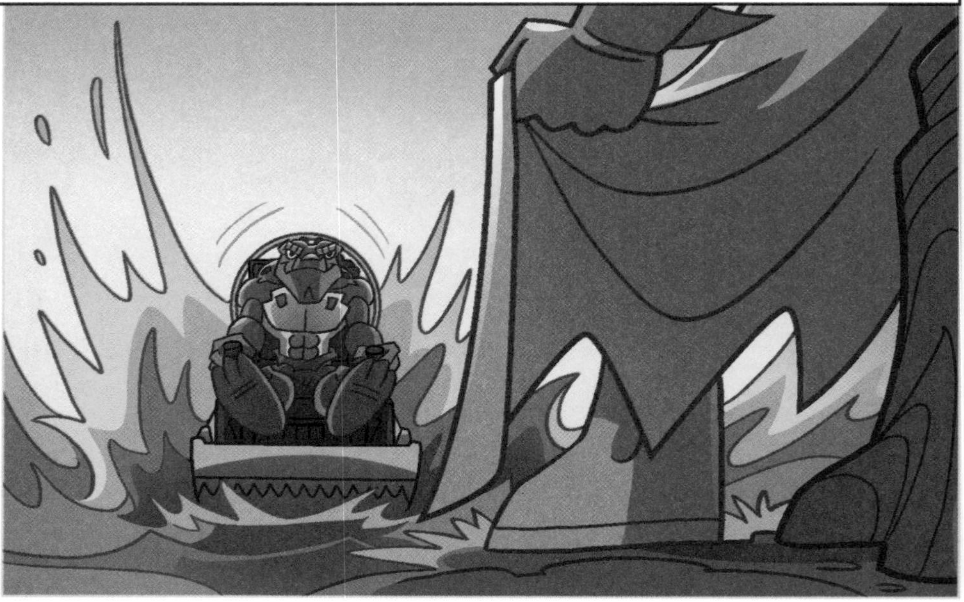

Croc crashes into a stump!

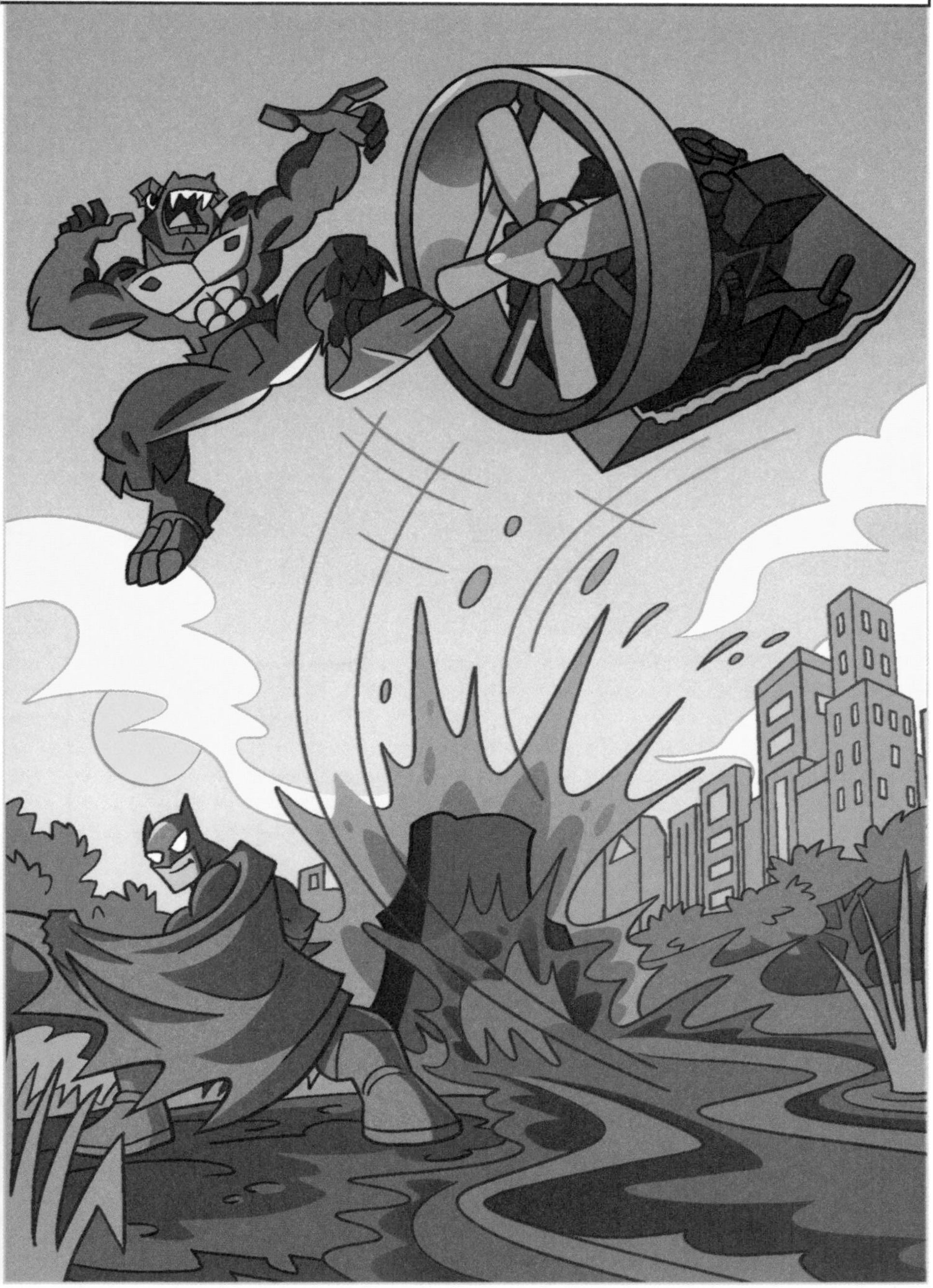

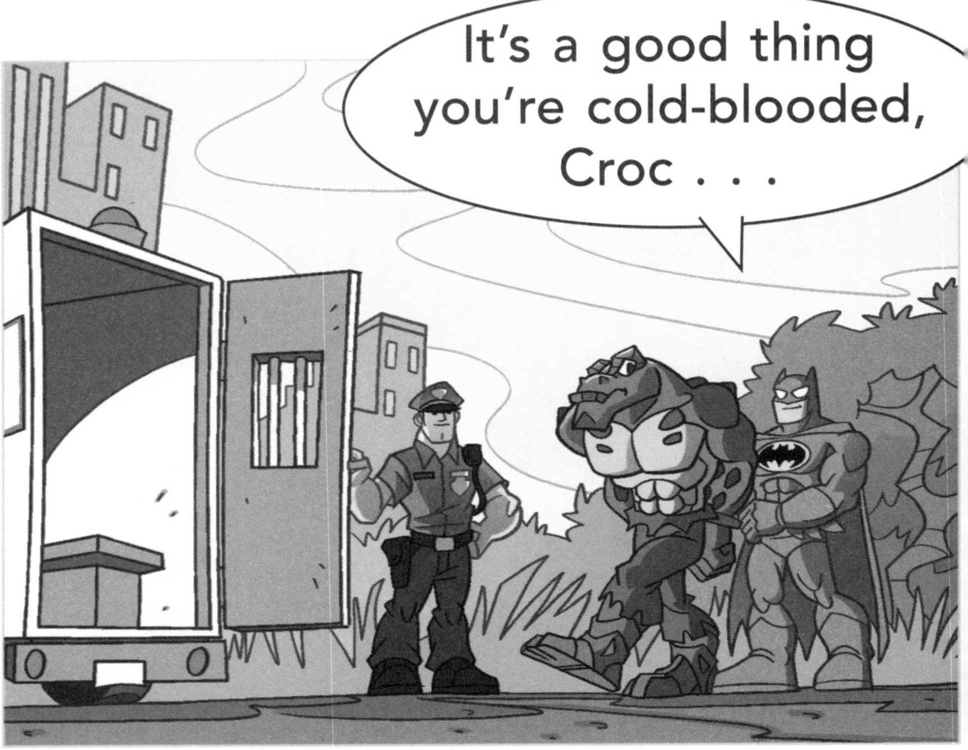
It's a good thing you're cold-blooded, Croc . . .

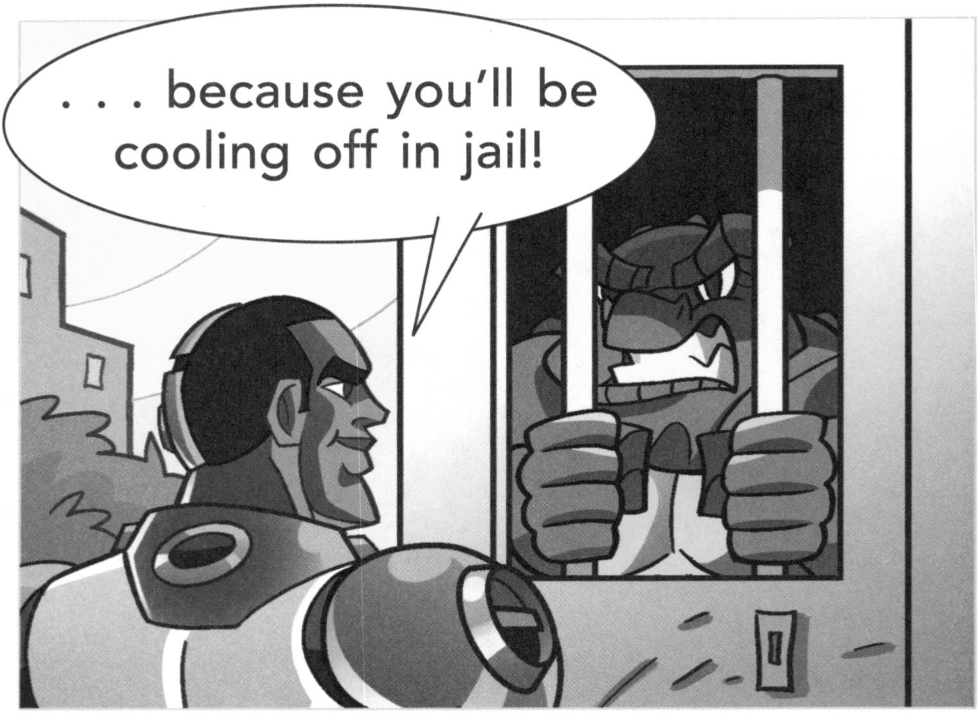
. . . because you'll be cooling off in jail!

Without Croc to command them,
the reptiles return to the swamp.

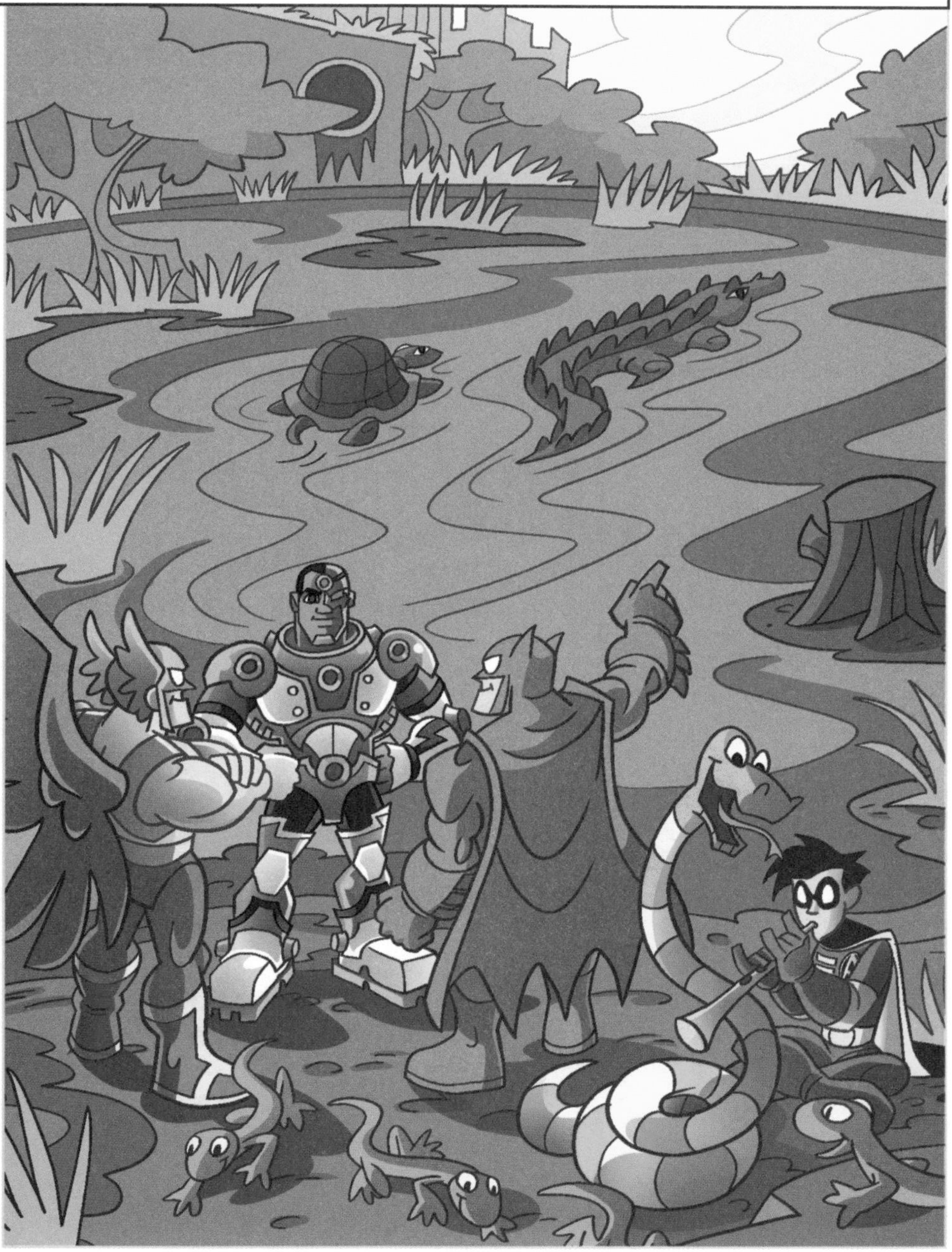

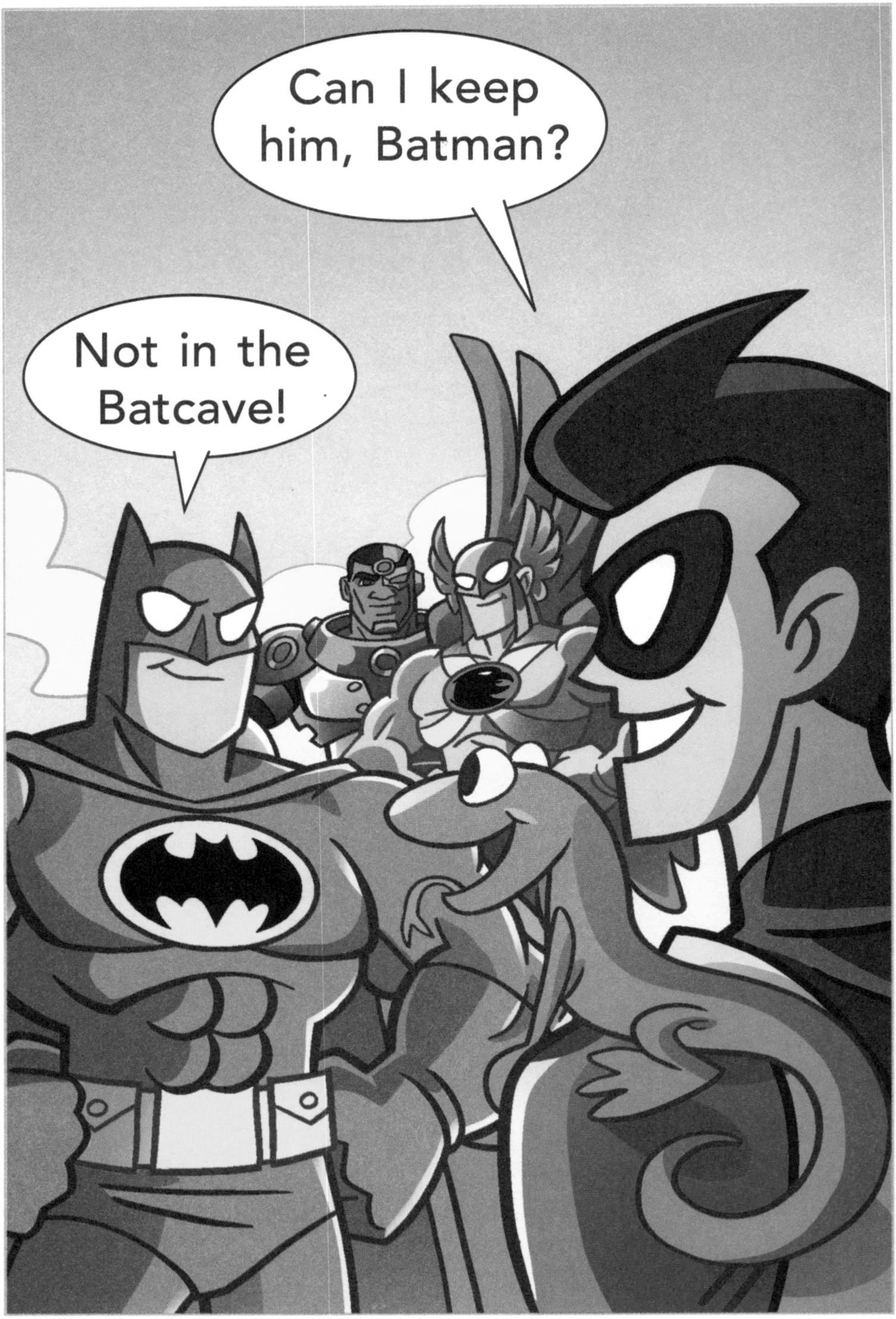
Can I keep him, Batman?
Not in the Batcave!